Alma

Alma was first published
in 2011 in Spanish by Lengua de Trapo,
© Javier Moreno

© of this edition, Quantum Prose, 2018

Editorial director
Marta del Pozo

Editorial advisors
Lissi Sánchez
Sarah Lipman
Nick LeBlanc
Gregg Harper

Cover by
Jesús Olmo

Designed and edited by
Hugo Clemente

ISBN
978-0-9973014-1-0

Library of Congress Control Number
2016933360

Quantum Prose, Inc.
New York, NY

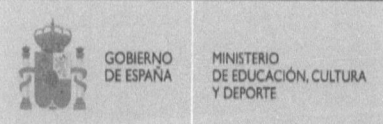

GOBIERNO
DE ESPAÑA

MINISTERIO
DE EDUCACIÓN, CULTURA
Y DEPORTE

"This work has been published with a subsidy from the
Ministry of Education, Culture and Sport of Spain."

Alma
Javier Moreno

Translated by
Peter Kahn

QUANTUM PROSE

Anecdotes are the only part of history that I love.

Prosper MÉRIMÉE

The rag-picker picks up what culture throws away, and sometimes found amidst the garbage are rags as valuable as humanity, subjectivity or depth.

Walter BENJAMIN

I am simply asking myself: Why a story at all-not that it was a bad story, or untrue, or that it debased anything. Why not, simply, the truth?

Doris LESSING

I REMEMBER MASTURBATING once, thinking only of myself, and I felt no pleasure at all. My fingernails have no ridges and shine as if painted with nail polish. I like Chinese food, Indian food, Italian food, Japanese food and Mexican food. I can competently cook at least half a dozen dishes from each of these cuisines. I don't know anything about Australian or Chilean cuisine. I eat everything except offal and organ meats. At one time in my life the Cathars seemed agreeable to me. When I was older I was surprised to discover that the world was full of them. When I was little I had flat feet. Maybe I still have them. As a teenager I had scoliosis. My anatomical correctness is artificial. I joke with my friends that I'm the Ana Obregón of orthopedics. I don't believe man will ever land on Mars. Until I was twenty years old I never wrote a single word that had anything to do with literature. I still don't really know what I'm talking about when I use that word. Perhaps it's best not to try to make literature. Just write, plain and simple. I learned to read and write when I was four years old. When I was five I wrote a letter to a girl in my class declaring my love and assuring her that we would get married when we were thirty. I still feel guilty about not keeping my promise. I started writing just to see what it was all about. I discovered that it was about many things. I'm not Colombian. I'm not the director of *El País*. I've never lived in Segovia. I'm not a soccer player. I'm not a cyclist. Melodies easily get stuck in my head but I almost always mess up when I try to sing a verse. At least twice in public I've confused the expression, "the miracle of the bread and fish" with "the miracle of the breast and fist." My favorite sandwiches are packaged ones you get at service stations. I prefer sandwiches made by others to ones I make myself. When somebody else makes them they have that added mystery of not knowing what's inside. To produce a mutation no cause is necessary. Causes are only necessary when you want things to remain static, immobile. When I eat meat I have to be careful not to get any sinew stuck between my third and fourth molars on the upper right side because when that happens it can be really painful. Beautiful people tend to come from dissimilar parents, one who's beautiful, the other not so much. With good books something similar seems to happen (this sentence sounds deliberately enigmatic). As it says in the Wen Fu, "By combining the popular Xia Li melody with the refined Bai Xue melody, we increase the greatness of both." I fantasize about writing a story in which the main character (female) keeps a scanned record of all her experiences (faces of lovers, theater programs, movie tickets, hotel towels, etcetera) and saves them on her hard drive in a folder called Alma. Standing in a crowded subway car I see less heads higher than mine than heads that are lower, from which I deduce that my height must be above average. I imagine that after death, to get into paradise, we'll all have to enter a password on a keyboard the way we do at the ATM. Only the chosen will be able to remember their password. I'd like to witness the moment of the resurrection, to see how atoms cluster together into particles and then accumulate until they form appendages that in turn join together to complete their original bodies. Van Gogh's ear will meld back into the rest of his head. I imagine the moment God presses the rewind button on his remote control because history has reached the end and he wants to watch it all over again from the beginning and forget once and for all the causal adverbial clauses. Just after I was born an inexperienced nurse put my crib near an air conditioner. When my father came in to see me, he found a baby that was turning blue and shivering with cold. I wish I could remember my father's face in that moment. I believe women are better long-range planners than men. I've never had a maid. One day an old woman stopped me in the street and asked me for some money to buy a bus ticket (she said her purse had been stolen). I gave it to her. It's hard for me to get drunk. I recover well from heavy drinking. I've never tried Alka-Seltzer. I'd like to write a story like *Against the Grain*, by Huysmans, with a character who rents a small studio with furniture that is one hundred percent from IKEA. The character would live almost his entire life connected to the internet, visiting extravagant pages—pages like words that appear only once in the dictionary and almost nobody knows. A digital sybarite. That would be the gist of it, the seed from which the character would grow in successive stages. I like aspirin. I like the groove drawn across the pill's diameter that makes it resemble the empty set symbol. The old woman I mentioned a moment ago asked me for money a second time for the same reason. This time I didn't give her anything. I sleep the sleep of the righteous. I suffer from bruxism. Bruxism is like rage, rage that keeps everyone safe and is only dangerous to oneself. If I were an artist I'd conceive of an installation composed of a house equipped with all the conveniences, almost blindingly illuminated with halogen lamps, furnished with the latest advances in automation. In the living room I'd paint a crevice in the wall. On the floor of the kitchen there would be a couple of small crystal urns. One would contain a live rat, the other would contain a cockroach (also alive). In the bedroom there would be a built-in cabinet with a glass case containing a moth (alive). In the perfectly sanitized bathroom I would put an air freshener. Every time someone pushed its button it would fill the air with a repulsive odor of detritus. My favorite chess piece is the knight. With the knight you can move everywhere on the board without landing on the same square twice. You can jump over the other pieces. Not even the king can do that. The knight is like the third dimension in chess. In writing, something similar happens. You can jump over coined phrases, over space and time: the third dimension of language. It occurs to me that this could be a good definition for literature. For a long period of my life I preferred long-sleeves to short-sleeves. When I was five I asked God for proof of his existence. I asked for loads of toys. They were supposed to appear in the morn-

ing at the door to our house if he wanted me to believe in his om-
nipotence. It goes without saying that those toys didn't appear.
Since then, not only don't I believe in God but I'm still a quite angry
at him. One thing's for sure: I could be the character in that Huys-
mans-style novel. On my bedroom wall there's a reproduction
(printed with a Canon Pixma 150) of Oedipus and the Sphinx by
Gustave Moreau. Moreau is a painter—in poor taste, who I really
like. In fact, the story about the girl who scans objects to convert
them into memories and the one about the boy who rents a small
studio apartment are suspiciously similar. They could become the
same story. Or at least the two characters could get to know each
other. She would have a lover named Darío who's a professional
photographer. She would scan his skin (his face, his butt, his hands,
the bottoms of his feet…) and she would contemplate those vestig-
es of that absent body as if they were the images of some badlands
on Google Earth. When I had a beard I stroked it constantly. Now
that I don't have a beard I don't know what to do with my hands. I
write. That I do. They once performed a scintigraphy on me. Until
I was ten years old I thought I could get pregnant. I avoided sitting
on any toilet where a fertile woman had recently sat, including my
mother. I have various explanations for this but almost all of them
are too philosophical to put down in writing. I stopped smoking
hashish several years ago. I was never very good at team sports.
When I played soccer I always played goalie. I was good. That's
what they said. I have good reflexes. I move quickly. I suddenly
appear next to people without them even noticing. Sometimes I
startle them. I think the two best pieces of Western music are Bach's
Erbarme dich, mein got, and Vivaldi's *Cum dederit…* I think having
two jobs is unbearable, unless one of them serves to forget the existence of the other. When I have to go to the gym I prowl around
like a caged animal, trying to put off the moment when I'll finally
have to leave and go back home. There's no place that I feel more

alone than at the gym. It's a fantastic place to disconnect the mind. To be only biceps, triceps, deltoids. To be only a body. At the gym people avoid each other's eyes like meteorites crossing paths in the void. The gym is a space of atrocious and devastating beauty. At the gym your degrees, the prizes you've won, are all unimportant. No intellectual merit is relevant. There you are just one more among many, insignificant amid the tons of steel subject to the tyranny of gravity, lying in wait for the beautiful bodies of athletes who try to defy it. You grab the weights and feel the force of gravity pulling your body toward the center of the earth. The gym is the closest thing to a communism of the body. It's becoming increasingly difficult to urinate in the street. Even the narrowest streets are now equipped with surveillance cameras. I've urinated under traffic lights, on tree trunks, into the sea, into a river, into a sink, on the windshield of a Mercedes, in the shower. I've never urinated in a doorway. Few things are as disagreeable as smelling the sweaty odor of someone in the audience attending the presentation of a book on aesthetics. I remember visiting the Barcelona Zoo as a child, but I don't remember having seen Snowflake. One of the good things about white shirts is that it's hard to notice dandruff on them. I really like white shirts. As a child I played at blanking my mind while staring out the window on public transportation. I think my life since then has been an attempt to fill those blank spaces. I hardly dedicate any time to the present. I am more interested in the present than in the future and the present less than the past. A friend said that to be Jewish consists in substituting the word yesterday for the word tomorrow and the verbs in the past for their equivalents in the future. I circumcised myself when I was twenty years old. I bled and then an enormous blister like a toad's wattle appeared just below my glans. I had to explain this to the doctors. It was my way of becoming a Jew. Of starting to write. In fact, the present is nothing more than the realization of a past possibility. The present, like a reflection in a mirror, doesn't exist. You can own a mirror but never the reflections that appear in it. I remember once cutting out pieces of continents from an atlas. If you turn the map of Madrid 180 degrees you get the map of India. When I was a kid I sent letters to the embassies of Japan, Mexico and India asking for information on their respective countries. The format was more or less like this: "Dear Ambassador, I am a boy from Murcia interested in the geography and thousand-year-old culture of your country…" The three embassies sent me tourist brochures which I read with much curiosity and excitement. I still haven't traveled to any of those countries. Hanging my laundry up to dry on the patio is a delicate operation that I try to do discretely. My salt shaker lasts months before it's empty while my sugar bowl is empty after a week. Logically, I deduce that life requires more sugar than salt to sustain itself. Writing is a kind of preparation for death. It's like taking a swim in the pool on the terrace before plunging into the ocean from the cliffs. Something similar happens with reading. Fragmentary writing allows you to come up for air every so often. Fragmentary writers have weak lungs or, perhaps, they're shy, unable to keep the reader's attention for very long. More than anything else they don't want to be annoying. Once, when I was a kid, I was playing with my cousin the way boy and girl cousins play. I undressed her and placed small pebbles taken from my grandparents' patio all over her body. On her head, on her outstretched hands, on her throbbing tongue and between the folds that, to my surprise, were between her thighs. I've always considered that to be my first work of art. The only thing that interests me in newspapers is the cultural supplement. I read the other sections as if they were short exercises in fiction. When I work out on my Exercycle I try to keep the needle past 120 watts. That's what four 30-watt light bulbs need to stay lit. I've never figured out whether window boxes should be hung on the inside or the outside of the balcony. I believe the human being is essentially a contemptible species and this is the secret of its evolutionary success. Between naivety and contemptibility I have always opted for naivety. I can't write the word *contemptible* without thinking at the same time of Thomas Bernhard. I roll and smoke my own cigarettes. Not like Des Esseintes' *paredro*, who only smokes Camels. Regular Unfiltered. He likes the camel stamped on the box, the aroma of Turkish tobacco. The cigarette between his lips is a metonym for the desert. Every time he lights a cigarette in his apartment, furnished exclusively with objects from IKEA, it seems to him that the walls frame a desert composed of a few square feet that only he is capable of exploring. In the supermarket I always end up in the slowest checkout line, with the least experienced cashier, the line where someone decides at the last moment that they don't really want the eggs or the batteries or a package of Kit-Kats. And then, typically, when it's finally my turn at the cash register, there are only one or two people behind me. I would never take a picture of a dead person. The girl who scans the events of her life and who, for the sake of convenience, we shall call María, scanned the corpse of a small hamster. The hamster's name was Pérez and he'd been her pet for a couple of years. He was a white hamster, so the scan didn't turn out as well as María would have liked. After scanning him, María put the hamster's corpse in an empty asparagus package. She closed the top and then sent it in a package to Calle del Arenal 8, 28013, Madrid. I'm not sure if the word *paredro* is in the Dictionary of the Royal Spanish Academy. I read it for the first time in a novel by Cortázar and I liked it. I think I know what it means. Sometimes certain expressions occur to me like "new religious talent" or "Russian roulette workshop," expressions which tend toward the absurd and that, beyond being laughable, could perhaps conceal some grain of truth. Someone said that to make people laugh it was only necessary to tell the truth. I think the comment is funny, so I suppose it must be true. When I came to live in Madrid my neighbor was Javier Marías. I'd read one of his novels without getting very excited. I ran into him on the elevator once, like any other neighbor. My penchant for mythomania has always been minimal. The Telepizza delivery boy would often make a mistake and knock on my door instead of Javier Marías's. I suppose the similarity of our names accounted for the confusion. I've never ordered a pizza by telephone, although none of my principles preclude me from doing it sometime in the future. After two years I decided to move out of that studio apartment. The building manager told me that Javier Marías was going to buy it and turn it into his library. And he did. I've recognized the wall of my former studio in a photograph of Javier Marías published in a well-known cultural supplement. I thought of leaving him a bunch of poems in the refrigerator. In the end I decided not to. I regret not having done so. I think it was Bolaño who kept his manuscripts in a refrigerator. But I didn't know that then. When I published my third novel I sent a copy to Javier Marías and a letter in which I told him this whole story. He responded by sending me one of his books as well as a letter. In it he said that my studio apartment had been too tiny for the purpose of enlarging his library, so he'd decided to rent another floor in the same building. I wonder who lives in that studio now. Some miserable wretch, no doubt. In fact, the cultural supplements have lost their importance. The cultural supplements are like the corkboard where you pin dried butterflies. It's obvious who the dried butterflies are. Eduardo, which is the name I've decided to give to my imitation Des Esseintes character, collects postcards of buildings that no longer exist. Among them is one that shows the Hiroshima Castle before the atomic bomb and another one of the Twin Towers when they were still standing. Eduardo has a predilection for objects that once were but are no longer, or that persist but are on the verge of disappearing. Etch-A-Sketch drawings and expired cans of bean stew, for example. Sitting in front of his computer, Eduardo looks at the postcard of the Twin Towers and he feels as if he's looking at the icon for the pause button. The planes brought down the towers and History started rolling again. If I were an artist I would draw the Boeing 747s as giant fingers, the giant fingers with which the god of history, returning from taking a break, pushed the play button and continued with the show. I've never seen anyone leave the bouquets of flowers we see on the sides of highways, marking where someone once crashed and died. After eating I like to know that there is coffee already made in the pot, even if it's a couple of days old. I always drink my coffee black. I've never used butter to perform anal sex. I lived in a house in front of which, five hundred years ago, the Catholic Monarchs used to parade. Sometimes, before I open the door, I imagine that I'll find them leisurely sitting on my living room sofa. I'm not good-looking. I'm not ugly either. I'd like to write a story about someone who commits suicide by taking tranquilizers while contemplating Jackson Pollock paintings. He would take one pill for every color used in the painting. There was a time in my life when I couldn't tell the difference between a work by Rothko and one by Pollock. A friend I may talk about soon, the same friend that enlightened me as to the true essence of Jews, told me that the two artists were hardly distinguishable except for the fact that one created his paintings with small splotches whereas the other used bands of color.

–Like the ones on some soccer jerseys?
–More like on flags. Imagine Rothko as a painter of flags, a painter of flags from countries we still haven't discovered.

Since then I can tell the difference between the two artists perfectly. I could lie down for hours listening to marine weather forecasts. Rough seas, hazardous seas, combined seas… These are terms brimming with poetry and mystery. I think the greatest curse is the one that says: may all your wishes come true. I like kind thoughts but I like geraniums more. I've seen faces in stucco walls. I can recognize no more than two or three constellations. I feel no pleasure when someone massages my feet. To make mistakes is the only way to be original. There have been periods in my life when, for no particular reason, I thought about suicide at least fifty times per day. I'm convinced I would never commit suicide. I imagine a guy who has gone completely crazy and is only capable of spewing social-democrat political discourses. I imagine that the entire population of the planet has gone crazy and is only capable of spewing social-democrat discourses: on the elevator, during family dinners, in line at the bakery. The social-democrat discourse would become something like the weather, the thing you talk about when you don't know someone very well, when you're not interested in knowing anything about him, when you don't want to keep quiet in the other person's presence and you don't want to look at the floor, you don't want to just haul off and wallop him. Ah, so much frustrated violence on elevators in the name of the weather. Elevators could become the ideal place for serving justice, as instruments they're akin to guillotines and scaffolds, places where truly democratic justice is carried out. After so many years, if I happened to run into Javier Marías in the elevator again, I think I would talk to him about the weather. I would say that it was truly awful outside, even if it was a gloriously sunny day. He would shrug his shoulders. I refer to the weather, I would add. He would respond negatively, that the weather was stupendous. I would tell him that I was referring to a different kind of weather, the weather for the arts, the weather in which dinosaurs like him and me were stampeding, in terror, toward extinction. His expression of astonishment would transform as irritation. Then I would push the stop button. Our scrotal sacs and his book-filled FNAC tote bag would rise for just a fraction of a second from sudden inertia. I would stand between him and the control panel and I would say to Javier, I want you to get naked, I want you to bare your soul to me, I want us to speak man to man, dinosaur to dinosaur. Then I would push the button for the fifth floor. Open your bag, Javier. I would say commandingly. After all, I was taller and younger and I smoked much less than the author of *A Heart So White*. Terrified, convinced that he had crossed paths with a dangerous lunatic, Javier Marías would open his bag and show me its contents. I would take it in my hands. I would rummage through the books until I found his translation of *Tristam Shandy*. Then I would raise it over my head, brandishing it like Moses with the stone tablets at the same time as I would say: This is the fifth floor, we are at the top. Congratulations, Javier, you chose well, you did the right thing. *Ego te absolvo*. Then we would go down to the fourth floor, and I would push the button with the number four. I would wave *The Sound and the Fury*, by Faulkner, in the air. We are idiots, Javier, we are like the idiot in this novel, idiots trying to decipher the background noise of existence, just like me at this very moment, convinced that I've turned this elevator into a literary system of coordinates. And I would take the opportunity to push button number three. Our homes, Javier, the intermediate point, the worst of all options. If only we had a dark basement, we could find some dignity in our misery, the dignity of a scream rising from the sewage. But no, here is where we get off. How sad, Javier. You don't know how many times I've wanted to ring your doorbell dressed as a Telepizza delivery boy to share all this sadness with you. And then I would watch as a tear would gradually form in his eye and run down his cheek until falling into his now empty FNAC tote bag at the same time as his chest would begin to heave at irregular intervals. I imagine the finale to this scene with us both ending up on our knees, our beating hearts synchronized, joined in an embrace. I believe you enter this life in order to become a story. I believe that the last thing our consciousness does before it dies out is to tell us the story of our lives. I wish I could record it and project it for anyone interested. It would be a film without copyright. The whole world could record a copy and save it on their hard drives. I like the idea that I could exit this world leaving behind a recordable *freeware* soul. I never wear sunglasses. I've never understood why the word *god* should be capitalized. *Never* is a word filled with mystery. *Never ever* is the greatest of mysteries, an expression upon which one could build a temple. The last thing I imagine before falling asleep is that I'm a soccer midfielder and I send crosses into the goal area that I score myself. It's fabulous to be Zidane and Maradona at the same time. When I was little, there was a show on television with a very serious man who would read sayings. I liked that program very much. I loved the sayings. When Franco died, the people around me were very upset. I didn't understand what was happening. My father told me that the man reading the sayings had died. That's what Plato called telling the truth with a lie. My father never read Plato. The name of the village where I lived with my family was La Cueva. Plato would not have approved. I left one cave to move to another. We never stop living in caves. I try to keep a cigarette lighter in every room, in every pocket of every jacket. When I look for a lighter, however, I can never find one. I tend to feel more comfortable with people who are older than me than with younger people. I admit to some exceptions. Some of the things we experienced in infancy are like the impressions of a negative on photographic paper that only appear after being left to soak for a very long time in silver nitrate solution: we have to let many years pass before we can see them clearly. Something similar happens with that painting by Monet entitled, *Japanese Bridge*, which can only be appreciated if we stand several feet away from it. I'm thinking of the landscape I would see through the window of the bus that took me to school. Now, thirty years later, I can see it all clearly. It's a truly beautiful landscape. There are lemon trees, palm trees, thickets of lemon clover growing on the banks of the ditches glistening with dew. There's a boy who doesn't know who he is yet, but to whom, little by little, I'm giving form. I'm a Virgo. In some sense, I believe in astrology. I see myself in the god Hermes. In the hospital, just after I was born, I opened my eyes often and stared intently at everything around me. If there'd been a cow nearby, I would have stolen it. I've consulted the Tarot and the *I Ching*. I've never eviscerated a dove in order to read the future. I like paintings more than photography, and photography more than architecture. I think film is a literary genre. I have an ambivalent relationship with music. Many of the things I say generally seem reasonable to me. I could even come to agree with some of them. I think it's terribly ingenuous to think that you have to do as you say. Cats are my favorite animals, immediately after humans. I've never voted for the same party twice. I don't remember how many times I've voted. More than two, less than five. Sometimes I don't know who I'll vote for until I close the curtain of the voting booth. I choose a slip of paper at random and put it in the envelope. If there were a category for "random vote," I would choose that one. To produce senseless noise, to imitate a force of nature, therein lies one of the few revolutionary gestures that remain within our grasp. I was allergic to dust for a while. I started to smoke when I was twenty years old. It was too hard for me to acquire the habit to give it up now. María thinks that to be in love consists in obeying one of the complex behaviors that are stereotypical of the arts and traditions and whose common denominator—except in the case of Platonic love—is undoubtedly having sex. According to my character María's theory, I've fallen in love with all the women I've ever been with except one. That's not because there wasn't any sex, it's because our relationship didn't correspond to any behavior that's stereotypical of the collective imagination. I want you to think of the barycenter of a wasp nest, of a desert island and a film by Godard. I've never managed to fill my grocery bag at the supermarket before the cashier announced the total of my purchase. "Emotional intelligence" doesn't even seem to me to be an interesting oxymoron. I detest political correctness. Every time I hear the term, "reach a consensus," I have an urge to pull out a revolver and shoot the next person who walks by. The last time I read a self-help book I was an adolescent. It was *The Greatest Salesman in the World*. I followed the instructions to the letter. I recited hundreds of sentences that were intended to inspire the reader—that is, me—and whose aim was to catapult him toward success. Sentences like:

Henceforth I will recognize and identify the mystery of moods in all mankind, and in me. From this moment I am prepared to control whatever personality awakes in me each day. I will master my moods through positive action and when I master my moods I will control my destiny. Today I control my destiny, and my destiny is to become the greatest salesman in the world! I will become master of myself. I will become great.

No matter how much I reread this stuff, I can't make any sense of it. Without realizing it Og Mandino wrote a surrealist book. *The Greatest Salesman in the World* is truly a fabulous surrealist book. I believe that self-help writing is the quintessential adolescent genre. Psychology is one of the spiritual evils of this decade. The only reasonable psychology is that which you can find in some novels. If someone were to ask me who god is I would answer that he is an important secondary character in the Bible. I could turn god into a character of this novel. He would be a secondary character, a character who would have to ask permission of everyone else to do anything, even to go to the bathroom. He would have the habit of going up to other characters and scolding them and telling them what they should do. He would be a guy who is determined to convince us that the conscience is a place full of rooms that should be kept clean (a place without ashtrays or wastebaskets) and that there is something called "I" that is condemned to live there—inside—until someone comes to rescue us and lead us to a door on which an invisible hand has written the word *paradise*. So, god would be a kind of psychologist. Yes, I'll probably end up making god into one of the characters of this novel. When you get right down to it, that's what he deserves. *Bach* means "stream." *Bach* means "stream." I've written it twice because it seems very important, considering how infrequent it is for there to be such a coincidence between a word and a thing. For the moment I'll return to Eduardo. Eduardo has some glasses that enable him to see reality as if he were observing it on the screen of a computer. With a button attached to one of the arms he can increase or decrease the pixel level, from the usual 1024 by 768 down to an elemental 1 by 1, which is something similar to colorful blindness. I've never heard or seen a radio or television recording in which I'm featured. I don't like to appear in any image if I'm not in control of the frame. I only look good in self-portraits. Writing is a kind of self-portrait. My hands are almost always cold. Literature is a kind of thought from which all definitive conclusions must be eradicated. Literature is the road that goes from zero to one, without including any extremes. Extremes are always intolerably vulgar. I've never bought any clothing in an exclusive boutique in order to go to a cocktail party and then return it the next day with the price tag still attached. I've never played Secret Santa. Whenever Eduardo leaves his apartment to run some type of urgent errand (to buy food or an ink cartridge for his printer), external objects seem to him to be cheap imitations of all those images he's seen on internet. *Alhábega*: I know what it means. I wonder what kind of film would be made by someone who could live two or three hundred years, I mean, what film would such a director make, what would the main theme be, how long would it be. What kind of film would god make?

–One that featured a single camera angle. A boy in a room

with white walls. The boy discovers his own image in a mirror. The boy lifts his arm and tries to touch his reflection. Recorded in ultra high-speed. The gesture is only completed after millions and millions of years. The final shot would contain the only vestige of order, the final image in a universe where entropy has triumphed and now offers the spectator (the same god or, perhaps, a different god) the white noise screen of an off-air channel.

    Eduardo has visited Armenia, Lapland, India, Australia, the Fiji Islands… All the places that Rimbaud clipped from his childhood Atlas and presumably wanted to visit. Eduardo sees himself as a Rimbaud in the era of internet. He visits all these places without the need to move from his Allak chair from IKEA. He knows that a typical Turkish dish is lamb stew with yogurt, cooked with olive oil and butter. After flying over the highlands of Anatolia with Google Earth, he prints an image of the lamb stew (size 12x25 cm) and carries it with him to the kitchen. He opens the cabinet and takes a can from an enormous stack of bean stew cans. Then he takes the image of the lamb stew dish and wraps it around the can of bean stew. Only then does he open it and eat directly from the can, without heating it first. I forgot to say that Eduardo only eats canned bean stew (past its expiration date). The average is always below average. I don't have a favorite movie. I lack continuity. I wish I was a little more saturnine. If I were an object of nature I would be more like a subatomic particle than a planet. Equations of a greater or equal degree than five are not solvable by radical numbers. Eduardo has a hard time accepting that human vision doesn't have a zoom function. I don't believe the universe is flat or hyperbolic or spherical. The universe is in no way fixed. We humans aspire to be more than one. It's not enough for us to be just one person. Hence our need to live adventures, to have two wives or two husbands or two jobs. Although ultimately this duality is unsustainable. The problem is that we humans are more than one but less than two. It has to do with a great gift and at the same time a terrible tragedy. I once dreamed that the sky was a great dome painted blue with enormous pockmarks in the form of clouds. I cried the first time I went to a discotheque. I was fourteen years old. I went there with my cousin and her girlfriend. I was surprised by how easily they fit in with the crowd in that noisy, smoky atmosphere. They'd already been there several times. They bought a pouch of tobacco and smoked cigarettes. I suppose the sensation was similar to that of a child's attending kindergarten for the first time. When I was a kid I rode a pony. It was a carnival attraction. I remember it smelled horribly, a combination of animal sweat and excrement. I remember its sad face. I discovered that reality has nothing to do with the images I'd seen on television. I rode around on it as if I was on a merry-go-round. For the entire ride I couldn't stop thinking about how sad that animal's life was. When it ended I breathed a sigh of relief. I was so sad I only wanted to go home. Memory is a plastic and infinitely expanding substance. Memory has a kind of zoom function. The greater the degree of enlargement the more one has to view memory as fiction and resort to one's rhetorical devices. Mastery resides in knowing how to use the zoom. I once ate a snail. I never ate another. Typing your own name on the Google bar to see the results is like looking at yourself in the mirror, a mirror that returns dozens of deformed reflections. If you have a strange last name you have more chances to triumph in life. There are statistical studies to support this claim. The same is true for animals. Purebred dogs and cats tend to live in better conditions than those that lack pedigrees. Unless you're a Roman cat. No animal in the world lives a better life than a Roman cat, be it a tiger in the jungle or Tinkerbell in Paris Hilton's pocket. There are very few attributes that persist in defiance of the inconstancies and quirks that make up life. This is something that the typical mortal refers to as character. According to some Australian scientists, light currently travels slower than it did several million years ago. The universe is getting tired. I once heard a nun tell a joke in which she used the phrase, "several million years." The nun had a good laugh after telling her joke. My friend, god, was there and he had a good laugh too. Nuns seem to be the happiest people in the universe. The happiness of nuns, unlike the speed of light, is increasing with the passage of time. A typical nun is happier today than two hundred years ago. I think it would be ideal to be a nun two thousand years from now. This is what I tell god but god doesn't laugh. All nuns read *El Mundo*. All nuns will go to Paradise. I don't read *El Mundo*. Therefore, I'm not sure whether or not I will go to Paradise. I ask my friend god about this and he shrugs his shoulders. He tells me that there's no logic in these cases. I tell him that the world could be a paradise, that this is what the Jehova's Witnesses go around professing. God tells me that first you would have to die and then be resuscitated. I tell him that that seems too conventional to me. In any case, I'd like to stay alive for a few more years even if the world and paradise remain separated by a bunch of dictionary words. I believe that we men enjoy orgasms less than we enjoy libertinism. The orgasm is a necessary conclusion, but what is more important is the path of tiny depravities that leads up to it. The orgasm pertains to nature, whereas libertinism pertains to culture. Plot has never been what drives my interest in novels. Animals don't seem to enjoy the act of mating. In those moments they appear to be slaves obeying the dictates of their physiology. This is the paramount reason why an animal cannot be depraved. This seems to me to be the clearest point of distinction between human beings and the rest of the animal world. Nature is boring. To recognize the truth in this statement and to act accordingly is what really makes us humans. The goal of narration, like that of the joining of bodies, is pleasure. Beatus of Liébana's Commentary on the Apocalypse of. John, or the *Commentarium in Apocalypsin*, says that at the end of the world the stars shall fall to earth like ripe figs from a fig tree. A cosmological image of the male orgasm. End of story. The end of all stories. I've never won the lottery. Christmas, like most endings, usually leaves me feeling sad. Christmas is a mini-Apocalypse. I don't wear rings. I don't wear bracelets. I don't wear necklaces. When I was eighteen years old I had four grey hairs. Now I couldn't hazard a guess on their number. Stephen Hawking confessed that, according to his editor, for every formula included in his book he would lose at least a thousand readers. I think the same thing happens with literary references. Unless you turn Dante or Homer or Borges into some kind of good-for-nothing and turn your own work into an enigma of universal proportions. I could turn this book into some kind of museum and bring together the greatest humanists, the greatest writers, the greatest artists of all time. Yes, I could do that, but others do that much better than I do. Anyway, I'm afraid they wouldn't find this book to be a very cozy place, they would end up being offended by one of my claims, by one of my phrases. I could speak about my fellow writers. I know quite a few. I could extol their virtues and reveal their shortcomings. Yes, I could do that. But that would be like judging the dinosaurs just before their collision with the meteor. A total lack of tact. Or perhaps the dinosaurs are already extinct and they, that is, we, are the creatures that have survived, grateful for our diminutive size, inhabiting a tenuous and violent world that scarcely tolerates us. I think I've already said this, but there are some things I never tire of repeating: plots bore me. The events in our lives only last for a few seconds; at most, for a few minutes. One line or one page should be sufficient for describing them. The rest—the plot—is nothing more than extrapolation. Life is a sum of events lacking plot. Perhaps we could say that there are minor convergences that give the illusion of meaning. I once discovered that a woman was cheating on me. It was in France. One afternoon I went to the supermarket. As I was returning home, bags of groceries in hand, I saw her from a distance. I'd bought her favorite jam. I'd bought red spinach. I'd bought a screwdriver (*tournevis à bout plat*) to fix the lamp on our night table. She was running. She passed no more than thirty feet away but didn't see me. I didn't say anything to her. I knew immediately that she was returning from a lover's tryst. I felt no hatred, no jealousy, but rather compassion. When I got back to our apartment she gave me a hug. Her heart was still pounding. I kissed her and prepared dinner. I put a saucepan filled with water on the stove and watched it until all the liquid had completely evaporated. As representatives of our species we writers should extinguish ourselves with dignity, we should look for a secluded place to leave our bones and let them dry. Not permitting the media to use our images should form part of our death with dignity. Every time a photograph of me appears in the media I feel that I'm betraying my species, that a writer is anything other than an image, that a writer writes precisely because he doesn't have an image. María collects old photographs, photographs that she finds at the Rastro flea market. They are poignant photographs, photographs that contain a story, photographs that are not made with silver salts deposited on cellulose but rather with words. Her search goes beyond the birthday pictures, wedding pictures, pictures of heads protruding from holes in cardboard sets on which someone has painted pictures of muscle-men or aviators in flight. As soon as María gets home with her photographs she scans them and saves them in the folder called Alma. Then she sends them to Eduardo, attached to an email in which she narrates a story based on the image that she makes up. Eduardo knows that the stories are fictions, but he doesn't care. They are (he thinks) like Ray Harryhausen's special effects, unable to make you forget the artifice that sustains them and, precisely for that reason, much more amazing than those produced with the most modern technology. I haven't mentioned, I believe, that Eduardo and María know each other.

They met in a stand at the Rastro flea market where they sell secondhand photographs and postcards. María was looking for old photographs and Eduardo was looking for postcards of buildings that have disappeared. They looked at one another, they stood side by side in front of the boxes filled with images, they even brushed hands in the frenzy of their respective searches. They still cross paths from time to time, on Sundays, in the same stand at the Rastro, although they haven't spoken. Eduardo doesn't know that the person who sends him the stories illustrated with images is María and María doesn't know that the person who receives them is Eduardo. They met on Facebook. They were both members of the group, "People who would prefer to be characters." The map of Spain has always seemed to me not to resemble the skin of a bull but rather the broken glass of a window with a view toward the center of the earth. In photographs of me as a kid I always have an angry expression on my face. That still seems to be the case. I've never understood why you should smile at the camera. With the passage of time, the lens has become a kind of eye from which nothing escapes, an unquestionable authority before which we prostrate ourselves wearing exhibitionist or submissive smiles. I've always looked into the camera lens with the same attitude as I would look at god if he were present: suspicious and distrustful. I've always sensed something. Something that has already happened. I hate taking out the garbage. There is nothing more decadent in these times than literature. And there is nothing more decadent in literature than subjectivity, that is, to speak of oneself. Literature is filled with subjectivity, with all kinds of people who want to talk about themselves, their preferences, their manias. It's repulsive but, nonetheless, it seems to be a symptom of our times. I'm far from being a subject. Perhaps I'm many subjects. We all have our own moment to appear, like the stars in the sky. I've been and I shall be Nietzsche trying to save the life of a horse. I am and I've been Rimbaud trafficking in slaves. I've been and I shall be that dog watching us and following us for a stretch of road until he gives up hope and disappears around the corner. I've been and I shall be something that happens too fast, ungraspable except in certain moments of ecstasy. The time it takes to change the share price of a company on the stock market. Something I still have yet to name. I once stood watching for minutes as the snow fell on a roof until the color of the roof turned white. What I like best about the body of a woman (not including her face) is not her breasts, her neck or ass, but her belly. I don't have a favorite fruit. I once found a human tooth on the beach at Cape Sounion. I thought about keeping it but finally my squeamishness got the better of me. I imagined it might be the tooth of an ancient Greek hero. I've never gotten rid of a book (not even the bad ones), although I know I should once in a while. I've never had a Scalextric brand racing set. The way I used to fantasize about committing suicide as a kid was by putting a large kitchen knife to my stomach and pressing with all my might. Then I'd imagine that the whole world would cry at my funeral and my parents would horribly regret not having satisfied my least desire. I suspect that everything we do in this life is meant to attract the greatest number of people to our funeral and to get those people to grieve and mourn our loss and feel deep down an irreparable sense of abandonment. I don't like my smile. Actually, what I'm trying to say is that I don't like seeing my smile, whether in a photograph or my reflection in a mirror. I once heard a conversation between two women. One said, "You have to try it again." The other one answered, "I can't." To which the other persisted, "You have to get to the end of it." The second one lowered her gaze and took refuge in silence. As in this case, there are many occasions when it is impossible to discern the sense of a conversation because we arrive after it has already started, because we lack context. I believe the same thing happens with everything, in general. For example, with a flower. No matter how much we observe it, it continues to be a mystery for us. We arrive in the middle of a story that began long ago, thousands or millions of years ago. The story of evolution. A story that no one can tell in its entirety. Someone sat us down in the auditorium after the movie began. We end up getting to know some of the actors, we get an idea of some strands of the plot. Nothing definitive. It's impossible to get to the credits. It's like coming out of the uterus and finding a world full of signs that we can't understand in order to try, little by little, to put some sense of order to this confusion of words and gestures.

> –I can help you a bit with things.
> –Do you know the context?
> –*Le context, c'est moi.*
> –A little bit of help is always welcome.

A baby is essentially a cryptographer. Nothing would please humanity more than the existence of something called *evil*, completely differentiated from something called *good*. Every civilizing impulse, all the walls and borders have been based on this artificial and, at the same time, necessary distinction. There is a good that must be separated from evil. I'm evil. You're good. Or the inverse. On almost all the webpages I visit I turn out to be visitor number 99,999. Once I discovered a feather in my hair. I don't know how it got there. I kept it for a few days. While walking to school I only used to step on the pavement stones that were sepia colored, avoiding the white ones. I don't remember the first time I drank beer. I've never taken an intelligence test. Not taking an intelligence test seems to me to be an obvious sign of intelligence. Regarding fiction, I confess that a moment has arrived in which I have given myself up to an insurmountable level of laziness. For example, to say that Eduardo went into the street one day and it was raining, so he was obliged to go back home to get an umbrella—something as simple as that—seems to me to be an inventive exercise that goes beyond my current abilities. What interests me is what happens when he discovers that he has forgotten his keys, his wallet and his cellphone inside his apartment, when for several hours he has to confront all by himself (he only has one friend in the city, and he lives too far away to be of any help resolving this problem in a few short minutes) an analog world in which, between zero and one, there's an infinite array of possibilities. An experience he hasn't been subjected to for several years. All of a sudden the group of beggars huddling in the San Andrés church doorway seems to Eduardo to be from another world. The beggars are breaking up pieces of wood to burn in a metal box. Now he studies their faces, lit by the flames toward which they extend their bare hands, and he senses that he is witnessing a Paleolithic scene. Eduardo is convinced that to start walking toward his friend's house could turn into an unthinkable adventure for a being so ill-suited to such an epic adventure. An odyssey devoid of the sublime. Something beyond his abilities. So, he decides to find a nearby locksmith. I think that I am at my best when I'm angry, when I deliver my counterpunch. Maybe that's why I never sidestep conflict. Few things are as disagreeable for me as a dog barking. Frequently people form a mistaken image of me and for this reason they speak or behave according to this prejudice and I, in turn, also feel obliged to conform to it. After taking out the garbage I feel liberated. On September 10, 2001, Michael Jackson performed his last live-broadcast concert. The following day two commercial jets, filled with passengers and crew, commandeered by suicide terrorists, brought down the Twin Towers. I believe that between those two events there lies a secret relationship which forms part of a single stitch in the inexplicable plot that weaves together World History. We could call this single stitch *The End of Pop*, or *The End of Postmodernity*, or *2001: A Space Odyssey*. There was a time when intelligence was necessary for the human being.

Men of genius were useful to humanity for a time in order to assure its survival. Once this objective was achieved, a man of genius was not only superfluous but he felt as poorly adapted to this world as a polar bear in a desert of sand. I've always been embarrassed about my muffin-tops. At times I think that one of the main goals of my life has been the elimination of my muffin-tops. I imagine the-day-after-the-elimination-of-my-muffin-tops as a kind of re-admission to Paradise. Without them life would lose a large part of its meaning. I'm fascinated by people who always think they're right. Language is filled with elegant words. *Right* is one of them. I think it would be more sincere to say that people want to get their way. More honestly, it would be even more correct to say that most people enjoy causing other people to trample on each other. It must be a vestige from when we competed for territory, females and the best hunting grounds. Wanting to be in the right is only a little better than wanting to carry a pistol, although the two are related.

> –*Right* and *arm* share the same etymology. They both stem from the Greek *ararisko*: to unite, to equip.
> –Sometimes I have an urge to believe in etymology.
> –I believe in almost everything. I even believe in you.
> –You flatter me.

Apparently, god resists playing a mere secondary role. It's nice to see forms in swirls of stucco or in the clouds, to forget that what's in front of you is a paint splatter or the condensation of water vapor. Naming things is a similar exercise. No one's aware that what they're seeing is an accumulation of matter formed by evanescent elemental particles. An object is the sum of all that we can't see in it, just as the fact that something that's the color red means that it contains the entire chromatic scale minus that which corresponds precisely to that particular color. We only see the remains of things, which seems intolerable to those very things. The rose is a waste product of the plough and the lips, of the mango and the mailbox, of the octopus and the microwave oven. It's in our dreams that we see what the mirror won't show us and what is, nonetheless, our very substance. That's why we never see ourselves in our dreams. If indeed we do appear it's in the form of a character, with a mask that's different from our pronoun. I've never understood the predilection for music. The fact that in the middle of a conversation people will begin to dance and sing strikes me as being as unnatural as the autobiography of a panda bear. I can't understand how it's possible that it has never occurred to any architect to construct a temple where, instead of saints on the façade, there would appear the effigies of the great civilizing heroes such as George Eastman, Albert Einstein, Tim Berners-Lee and Stanley Kubrick. The movies they show us on buses are worse than the ones they show us on trains which are worse that the ones they show us on airplanes. I have no idea whether astronauts watch movies on their space missions. They should pass a law according to which the quality of fiction increases the farther one travels away from the terrestrial core. The angels in heaven would see the best shows, the feature presentation of Paradise. The best books, the most realistic, are those in which someone has gone over them with an eraser until the plot has disappeared. Eduardo remembers an event as a child, an unforgettable experience, the only one in his life that was truly magical. He was eight years old and he was awake on Twelfth Night. It wasn't his excitement over gifts that kept him awake. At that age he already knew that the Three Wise Men were really his parents. Very simply, his dinner hadn't sat well with him and, tired of tossing and turning in bed, he got up to go to the kitchen for a glass of water. Barefoot, he walked over the parquet floor, groping in the dark (he didn't want to alarm his parents by turning on a light) until he made his way to the kitchen and filled a glass of water from the tap. As he was drinking he heard a noise in the living room, as if someone were forcing open the glass door to the balcony. He left the glass on the counter and went to the kitchen door. The kitchen led directly to the living room so that, standing on the threshold, he could watch as three men dressed as the Three Wise Men opened the glass door and entered the room. He could hear the rustle of their robes in the silence of the night. By the fireplace they left some packages before leaving the room by the same door through which they'd entered. Eduardo waited until they were gone. Then he returned to his room. In the middle of the hall it occurred to him to stop in front of the closed door to his parents' bedroom. Gently he placed his hand on the doorknob and slowly turned. Despite the darkness he could see the two mounds resting under the sheets. Surprising as it might seem, Eduardo returned to his room and fell asleep as soon as he lay down on his bed. The next day he opened the packaged gifts. Among them was an Etch-A-Sketch. An uncountable number of times I've walked down the street without realizing my fly was open. I believe the key to happiness is to live beneath your potential, which is often difficult to do. I feel a kind of embarrassment when I listen to the messages on my answering machine, as if I were listening to messages that someone had sent to another person. I have a large scar on my right eyebrow that adds asymmetry to my face. I know what it's like to do a barrel roll in a car. Once, at a book presentation, a photographer armed with her camera was lurking around the table where the presentation was being held. The area for the public was kept in virtual darkness. As I was speaking I was aware of her slipping among the shadows in a way that struck me as very sensual, blinding me occasionally with the flash of her camera. I could only make out the yellow color of her sneakers. The same sneakers Uma Thurman wore in *Kill Bill*. The first thing I do every morning is check my email. I check my email an average of forty times per day. I like the smell of fresh sweat in a woman's armpit. I like the sense of strangeness you feel when you join a conversation already in progress. I haven't seen any of the films in the Star Trek saga. "I prefer imagination to fantasy," is a stupid comment and yet it seems to contain an element of truth. There are some true statements that defy proof. Idiocy is an infinite realm that is in constant expansion and threatens the existence of humanity. I remember when my favorite color was red. If humanity had not dedicated so much time to reading, the world would be much worse than it currently is. If humanity had dedicated more time to reading, the world would also probably be worse than it is at this moment. As the Twin Towers were collapsing I was drinking a martini with a friend. A moment before turning on the television my only concern was to capture the olive beneath the ice cubes. I collect puzzle pieces. The only ones of any value are the singular ones I find on the ground. Surprisingly, the world, for those of us paying attention, is full of puzzle pieces. María has organized her folder, Alma, in the following way. By double-clicking we find a series of sub-folders. Among them are some with the following titles:

–Scanned things that look like an arthropod (among them, the scanned images of a feather duster, a Christmas star and a barette).
–Scanned things that look like an elephant swallowed by a snake (among them, page 34 of *The Little Prince*, a friend's bowler hat and a used condom).
–Scanned things that look like a Rorschach test ink blot (among them, a chocolate elephant ear and some panties with garters).
–Scanned things that look like Christ the Great Power (the cover of a CD coated with cocaine residue).
–Things that look like a CD (among them, several CDs).
–Scanned things that look like a dandelion seed after being caught between two fingers (among them, a pom-pom and a picture of a collision in a particle collider).

–Scanned things that look like a puzzle piece (a piece of gum, a piece of dead skin).
–Scanned things that look like a scar (a magnolia leaf).

María has a scar the length of her side, from her waist to her armpit, as if someone had tried to open her body and empty it, or to empty it and then refill it with something other than normal organs. Sometimes, when she undresses, she runs the tip of her finger along the scar and feels a strange pleasure. Touching her scar reminds her of the soft unevenness of her laptop mouse. She imagines herself clicking on her scar and being transported to some nonexistent place on the web, a place of pain, convulsion and shuddering. I think pornography is like those flowers that are able to confuse insects into believing they are copulating with another of their own species, or like the cotton in a glass jar through which it is possible to watch a seed grow. We live surrounded by fiction. So much so that fiction has become superfluous, unnecessary. We return home, wipe off the street advertising on the doormat and turn on the television with the burning desire to see someone tear open their chest and show us their guts. I used to despise lawyers. Now I find them reassuring. A lawyer is insurance against shams and impostors. The lawyer who appears on the television screen, certifying that the guts we see spilling from an open belly are really the guts of the gentleman accompanying them… can only guarantee his word if a second lawyer certifies that we have before us a trustworthy lawyer, an affirmation (that of the second lawyer) that should be certified by a third lawyer. Ad infinitum. The two-dimensional screen is a place of deception, or the possibility for deception. At this point I find it impossible to believe in any image. The image has lost its iconic value and has recovered its former symbolic and indicial value. Perhaps that's why María scans old photographs of people who have disappeared, because the photographs on their antique support of photographic paper are doomed to disappear, whereas their digitalization renders them everlasting. We could say that María grants those faces—staring implacably, with a mysterious air, or just stupidly—a semblance of immortality. Nothing would please María more than for her Alma to become immortal. I have never prepared a doctoral thesis. *Excremento* is one of the most beautiful words in the Spanish language. It's a word rich in tone and ripe with poetic resonance. If a book contains the word *excremento* it immediately gains value as far as I'm concerned. There's something beautiful about the idea of excrement that I don't care to analyze because in a certain way that would diminish its charm. I am not a first-born son. I like letting my nails grow. One day, sitting at his computer, Eduardo heard an enormous explosion. The window-panes facing the street rattled. One of them broke. Through the empty space of the broken window he leaned out and saw two or three train cars toppled over on the tracks. It was as if a mischievous child of uncommon size had pounded the train until it had been reduced to a twisted mass of smoking iron. Eduardo turned around, sat before the keyboard of his computer and typed into his search engine, "bomb attack Atocha station." There were no results. Then he noticed something strange. Stuck to the wall was something that had not been there just a few seconds earlier. It looked as if someone had squashed a giant insect against the wall. It was clear that it had entered through the empty window or it had hit the window with such force and velocity as to have passed right through and struck the immaculate white wall. Eduardo immediately understood what it was. He wasn't sure what he should do about it. He could call the police. He could clean it up and get rid of those human remains, by throwing them into the garbage, for example. Eduardo could not remember ever having felt so disconcerted in his life. Eduardo found himself confronting a moral dilemma for which no one had ever prepared him. He reviewed the lessons he'd been taught by his parents, his teachers, the movies and novels and videogames he'd seen, read and beaten. Like the search engine, his perplexed brain yielded no results. It's true that that tiny human fragment could, in the hands of the police, provide a clue of enormous value. Then he realized that even larger fragments from the same body would have remained strewn around the wrecked cars. At that moment Eduardo recalled a poem by María Auxiliadora Álvarez:

> *A heart exploded*
> *attains the most dissimilar forms*
> *and infinity*
> *the particles of a heart exploded*
> *settle down*
> *softly alighting*
> *choosing final residence.*

In fact, it was perfectly possible that the fragment would not be relevant and the police and ambulances would be too busy to be distracted by such a thing. On the other hand, there was the family of the victim. Although there was also the possibility that the piece of flesh belonged to the killer rather than the victim. That complicated things even more, if that's possible. Having reached no logical solution, Eduardo, like a robot marooned on an extraterrestrial surface, cut off from ground control, decided to act on his own. With a pair of tweezers from the bathroom he removed the organic remains from the wall and carried them to the kitchen where he carefully wrapped them in transparent plastic film. He opened the freezer and set the remains on the thick layer of ice that was threatening to occupy all the space in the refrigerator. Eduardo thought he had finally found a use for the freezer. The fact that he survived exclusively on cans of bean stew meant that he could dispense with that appliance. At first Eduardo thought this would be a temporary solution and that with the passage of time a reasonable way to resolve this upsetting problem would eventually occur to him. On the contrary, as time passed and events played out, Eduardo found it increasingly difficult to turn back. So, he simply left things as they were. From time to time Eduardo opens the freezer door and, now half hidden by the frost, he catches a glimpse of the human flesh remains which have now acquired a relic-like status. A day on which I don't receive a single email is a sad day. I don't know how to skate. When I was a kid I had trouble rolling my r's. One of my teachers once punished me for an entire recess period, making me sit at his desk imitating the sound of an engine in reverse while he corrected workbooks. I believe that since then I've pronounced my r's more than correctly. When I was twelve my mother took me to an endocrinologist because of my weight problem. The endocrinologist made me go into a small cubicle next to his office. He made me get undressed. He looked me up and down and then said to me, in a tone of voice filled with disgust: "Do you really want to look like shit your whole life?" There was a mirror in there. He made me ashamed of my body, of that vaguely anthropomorphic figure staring back at me with its boxers crumpled around its ankles. After a few months, I returned to normal weight for a boy my age. My teacher and endocrinologist weren't thinking about this boy's psychology. My teacher and endocrinologist probably didn't believe in psychology. They believed that things had to be done in a certain way and they acted accordingly. My teacher and endocrinologist taught me something important about life and about myself without the need for self-help books. I believe that any culture, any civilization, is unsustainable without some minimal aristocratic values. Spain is a country where all traces of aristocratic customs have disappeared. Spain is a country where mediocrity has settled in, completely at its ease, a country where mediocrity will remain to dwell unless it takes a hankering to travel and go to other countries. The first thing that is endangered when a country becomes absolutely mediocre is democracy. A mediocre people becomes a debased mass that can only be seen as clowns and psychopaths. I imagine a work of art that is a dandelion-seed dispenser. The viewer would use a keyboard attached to a computer to write a wish and, once entered, the dispenser would eject a dandelion seed enclosed in a semi-transparent globe, like the ones you can get at service stations containing panties and leopard-design thongs. People would take the dandelion seed between their fingers and blow on it to make their wish come true. Naturally, the title for this work of art would be *The Wish Machine*. I once saw a group of people huddled in the middle of the sidewalk, watching something. I followed the direction of their gaze to a man who had a dog on a leash. The animal was defecating against a wall, but standing upright on its hind legs in the position of someone who was being frisked by the police. When I pass through residential areas in a city I'm overcome by a sense of desolation. The geometric alignment of buildings, one after another, is the opposite of poetic language. Any one of those buildings could be demolished without compromising the rest in the least. Interchangeability is the fundamental concept of modern urban planning. Something that could easily be extended to sociology. I wouldn't like to see a photograph of my face in the moment I have an orgasm. Arthritis has deformed the joints of my middle finger on my left hand to the point that it resembles a small trefoil knot. I've always wondered if, in the earth's atmosphere, the number of low pressure areas coincides with the number of high pressure areas. I don't know how tall I am exactly. I never weigh myself. I never take my blood pressure. I'll never be able to forget the smell of just-skinned rabbit meat. God has a genuine passion for signing autographs. His strange mania drives him to attend all artistic events, all openings, in search of admirers. God is convinced that he was once a really famous person. Pausing in front of a painting by an avant-garde artist, surrounded by people, god isn't upset by the fact that he doesn't understand at all what he's looking at, but rather that no one is coming up to him to ask him for his autograph. God looks around him, he puts on a friendly smile in an attempt to avoid the slightest appearance of arrogance or aloofness, but the public doesn't seem to recognize him. He believes that, in spite of everything, he has managed to conserve part of his extraordinary aura all through time. One day while I was walking down the street I saw someone dressed up as Mickey Mouse. Surrounded by children with their hands outstretched toward him, the man dressed as Mickey Mouse signed a piece of paper and handed his autograph to the nearest child. I approached the man to ask for an explanation. God, I said to him, I know you're hiding in that disguise. The man dressed as Mickey Mouse instantly put away his notebook and hurried away down the street, occasionally hopping like a real rodent. I don't know what writer's block is. If I write I don't get blocked. If I don't feel like writing, I don't feel blocked in any way. My shoe size is forty-one. The number of questions one can formulate exceeds the number of answers one can give. Thus, it may be concluded that life is inextricably bound to enigma. I remember my childhood as constant boredom during which I wondered what I was going to do with time which, in that moment, I imagined to be infinite. I believe that being an adult consists in filling all that empty time of childhood. Every so often god turns on the television and inserts a copy of *Being John Malkovich* in the DVD player. God has been fascinated with that film since the first time he saw it. Since then he has seen it innumerable times, every time in a different language. God believes that he is the real protagonist of that film, that the screenwriter somehow knew of his existence and covertly reflected this knowledge in the story. Or that, in some way that is incomprehensible to god, the screenwriter was gifted with god's own gift. This gift has to do with the activity that brought fame to god in the first place, at some time in his past life. This gift, as he himself tells it, consists in his ability to visit the consciousness of another person, to infiltrate another's mind in order to live their experiences, to influence and direct them through their own thoughts. God is convinced that if he manages to see the film in all possible languages he'll gain access to the code that is hidden in the images and dialogues. Naturally, god doesn't understand the dialogue when it's dubbed into Russian or Chinese, but he believes that this lack of understanding constitutes part of the mystery that he has set out to decipher. Every time he gets to the credits of *Being John Malkovich*, god has the sensation of having been expelled from Paradise. I myself have witnessed god engaged in this kind of mind invasion, the signs that give away the fact that he has moved into someone else's consciousness. In these moments, god's gaze wanders, that is, he gazes upward at some indefinite place on the ceiling, as if he'd noticed a humidity stain or a spider, and at the same time he begins to utter an intelligible sound, something like, "bab-a-bab-a-bab-a..." God temporarily becomes a kind of celestial relay station sending an unknown signal to the endless universal void. I've never been a guest in a five-star hotel. Sometimes phrases pop into my head like, "the cellophane of the clouds." Then I wonder if it's possible that I might have heard someone close to me say the phrase in question during the day or perhaps I might have read it in some book months or years ago. I almost never find a convincing answer to this mystery. When I was fourteen years old I read *Dianetics* and *The Greatest Salesman in the World*. *Engram*: I know what it means. I remember having to write as a child, "I will not laugh at others," at least a hundred times. When you squeeze a lemon peel the tiny bubbles that are contained within explode and liberate a bitter liquid that is especially interesting when combined with the flavor of gin. I don't believe in reincarnation. I've never read Mendel's Laws. Dancing is not for me at all. It's impossible for me to leave things until the last minute. I believe that, in some way, writing is similar to playing the piano. What's important is to maintain the rhythm and not play out of tune. Every time I start a new page it's as if life had granted me another chance. Nothing is more unsettling for me than Nature. I wonder if it's possible to disguise oneself as someone who isn't disguised. I think the answer to the previous question has to be affirmative, in the same way that you can be, even without realizing it, someone you really aren't. Presenting a book is the closest you can get to a blind date. I am increasingly interested in, not movies, but rather, the ellipses that movies contain. The cuts that enable them to change scene or characters or temporality and that constitute the essence of the montage. When I watch a movie I try to imagine the story exactly as it is happening as if the ellipses had nothing to do with its production. The most impressive movie, without a doubt, is *2001: A Space Odyssey*, when the hominid launches the bone into the air and all of a sudden the bone becomes a spaceship plowing through space. What happens in that long interval of time is the history of humanity. Nothing more, nothing less. All history books are, without realizing it, attempts to come to grips with this ellipsis which leapt from the mind of Stanley Kubrick.

–Daniel Richter.
–What?
–That's the name of the actor who played the ape. The most famous unknown actor in film history.
–And what happened to him?
–He went to live with John Lennon and Yoko Ono. When they'd been drinking, in their house in New York, Yoko and John asked Dan to perform the Moonwatcher scene.
–And what did he use for the bone?

–A hammer. A hammer that he used to smash Beatles records.

Almost always, when it is said that someone has talent, what is meant is that the person is capable of virtuosity. Virtuosity is rare, but much less rare than talent. A virtuoso is like the monkey at the carnival that's able to behave like a human to the point of being indistinguishable from a human. The virtuoso is the perfect imitator. The virtuoso and the talented person may be similar, but they can never be confused. If the two of them are placed at the edge of the void, only the person of talent is able to bridge it. The virtuoso will fall to the bottom like a piece of lead. I remember my childhood as a paradise of infinite solitude. From cats you can learn pride and elegance. From dogs you can learn humility. Things that generate an immediate sense of sadness: a goldfinch in a cage, a stray dog, a flock of birds migrating at the end of summer, an empty mailbox. Once I saw a nun in the street and I fell in love with her immediately. I was struck by her black habit, absolutely anachronistic in the middle of the Latin Quarter. Her skin, so pale, glowed in the light of a radiant March day. She looked like she'd come out of a painting by Zurbarán, though Zurbarán didn't paint nuns. One day, at an art exhibit, I went after a girl in the gallery who was truly beautiful and I made my way toward her as if the painting she was looking at on the wall really interested me. At the last moment she turned around and I danced around her just before our bodies collided. As a result of this maneuver I managed to get directly in front of the painting. I can't remember what the artist was trying to express in that painting. Art almost always loses when it makes a deal with life. I have the impression that Gaudí, Tàpies and Barceló are three incarnations of the same artist. I believe that most of us human beings are incredibly clumsy. Although we can survive in a vast variety of environments, only in a few environments do we survive with any degree of grace and poise. Those few environments—very often just one—constitute our true habitat. I'm incapable of getting hooked on a television series. I don't use perfume. I've gone out of the house wearing kohl on my eyes. I think that one of the writer's duties is to scandalize others so they can reaffirm their good behavior. I have nothing against either one, neither against scandal nor against good behavior. When I wake up in the morning, for a minute I grumble about almost everything. I call it the minute of the damned. I'm anxious by nature. I write anxiously, I shave anxiously, I smoke anxiously. Writing the word *anxiety* does nothing to mitigate my anxiety. I think that in the white race beauty reaches its apex in women, whereas in the black race beauty stands out in the physical exuberance of men. Ego is a kind of wavelength, capable of being in many places at once, of occupying various positions. External pressures (family and peripheral violence) can concentrate this wavelength to the point at which it becomes a particle of extreme solidity. This was the situation until the middle of the last century. Current well-being and a lack of general external pressure (at least in Western countries) have restored the ego to its previous dissolute and wavering state. In a nutshell, a self is a stressed-out multiplicity. A stressful mortgage. A stressful job. A stressful wedding ring. Some friendships grow out of the most stressful situations. When I was a kid I would run circles around myself for fun until I was so dizzy I would fall to the floor. Just like electrons in their orbits. Just like galaxies. My conclusion is that children know something about electrons and galaxies, something that's not written in any physics textbook. Our civilization has replaced the obscenity of nudity and sex with the obscenity of death. I once saw three people walking in a forward slouch just like orangutans but without touching the ground with their knuckles. It was at an exit from the metro. It wasn't a happening. They didn't know each other. The three of them simply had the same defect and coincided at the exit of this station. Culture probably shortens the duration of moments of ecstasy, but undoubtedly contributes to their multiplication. Eduardo only eats food after its use-by date has passed. What I mean is that all his cans of preserved food are expired. Sometimes the use-by date is only a day before he consumes it, sometimes a week. Eduardo has proved that you can eat a can of bean stew that expired months ago. On rare occasions the contents of the can have really gone bad. He can count the number of times on the fingers of one hand that he has been obliged to throw one of his cans into the garbage. To eat food past its expiration date seems to Eduardo to be a poetic act. He feels a special satisfaction when he eats products that already exist, so to speak, in the past. Like the light that reaches the Earth from the stars, like the placenta in anti-wrinkle creams. In some way, Eduardo's behavior can be compared to the practices of certain religious sect members, like the Jains who try to reconcile life with the minimization of harm caused to Nature. In Rome, my wife and I were approached by a man who was completely drunk and wanted us to pose with him for a photograph. Another man, a very short one with a moustache and dark skin, stalked us from behind a camera with a disproportionately large lens relative to his size, while the drunk threw his arm around us. We posed as if we were all the best of friends. Like seasoned pets before the eager documentary lens. The drunk, who was an enormous pale blond man, around six-and-a-half feet tall, had to make a great effort to lower his head and rest it beside my ear without losing his balance. Two or three times he muttered a phrase in an unintelligible language that I freely translate as expressing gratitude for our having consented to pose for the photograph. He repeated, over and over, one word, something like *obstot*, a word that I can only transcribe with great effort into our Latin alphabet, a word that, like the majority of the words in that language I don't even know, must be written using an alphabet composed of splintering branches and oars splashing in a sea of freezing water. When we left the bar the albino giant had disappeared. The photographs of our smiling faces lay abandoned on the bar along with a mass of empty glasses. When María stares at the clouds she sees nothing. I don't mean that she doesn't associate the forms of clouds with something concrete; rather, she associates them precisely with nothingness. María looks at a cloud and contemplates the exact form of nothingness. Whenever I travel somewhere I photograph the most beautiful girl I cross paths with in the street, in a museum or in a plaza. When I travel and stare out the window of a train or an airplane all kinds of ideas occur to me that I later forget. I should carry a small notebook with me to record those impressions, but I don't feel like it. I think forgetting is one of the fundamental components of literature and, in general, of art. When I was twenty years old I read a book by Paul Auster whose title I don't even remember. I didn't like it at all. The title might have been, *The Country of Last Things*, or maybe not. Probably, if I read a book by Auster now, I'd find it interesting. It's even possible that I'd like it. That is something, however, that I have no intention of doing. Like so many things in life, whether one likes Paul Auster or not is a matter of choice and I have decided to live in a universe in which Paul Auster is, in no way, a relevant author. Here is one of the email messages that María sends every so often to Eduardo:

I WAS LUCKY THE OTHER DAY. I found a postcard with the first daguerreotype on it. You can see a person in it: one man, resting his foot on the fountain of the Boulevard de Temple. It's Hector Berlioz. Berlioz had developed the habit in his youth of getting up very early and taking a long walk before breakfast. After returning from Italy, the composer moved into a house located a couple of blocks from the Boulevard. During those walks Berlioz enjoyed the sensation of being alone in the world. That's how he composed many of his works in his head. Berlioz believed that a musician should compose as if he were alone in the world, as if he were the lone survivor of the apocalypse. In the improbable event that he met up with another member of his species, he would not speak (language would be useless in this case); instead, he would perform his music. He would hum a few measures of his Symphonie Fantastique and then turn and walk away. He would leave the other alone with his music. That's all.

ABOUT MARÍA'S PHYSIQUE, it's enough to say, for the moment, that she has a Romanesque nose set in a face that is so pale that it recalls the deathly sheen of white sheets hanging on a brick terrace under a cloudy Antwerp sky. I remember my childhood as a hell of infinite solitude. I find it extraordinarily pleasant to open my closet and suddenly discover some clothing whose existence I'd completely forgotten about. In those moments, when I put it on, I have the sensation of trying it on for the first time. When I have nothing to do I get very nervous. I'm terrified that something terrible is happening, that I've forgotten to do some ineluctable task, that my inactivity is due to some horrible carelessness on my part. Sometimes I propose stupid challenges for myself, like trying to hold a conversation using only words of less than four syllables, or words—excluding monosyllabic words—that are not stressed on the last syllable. There are so many books and so few readers that, in the face of such a disproportionate relationship between supply and demand, I believe a professional reader could become immensely rich. I imagine a kind of Bartleby whose job would be to read the books that no one has ever read. The smell of incense in churches automatically makes me think of death. When you've only seen someone in photographs and then you meet them in person you can't avoid appreciating the photographed face of the person instead of their real face, at least for a certain period of time. This proves that reality always lags behind imagination, kind of like the Doppler effect. I've never seen a dodo bird. Dodo birds are extinct. *Extinction* is a word with a tremendous future. Standing, with my legs straight, I can touch my palms to the floor. I used to have a beard; I used to have a moustache. Most of the time I've had neither one. The first time I masturbated I did it unconsciously. I bumped my penis and, worried, I was afraid I might have damaged it in some irreparable way. I was about twelve years old. At night, under the sheets, I rubbed it uneasily in pursuit of the desired erection. I was so intent on my endeavor that something quite unpredictable happened. A liquid from who knows where suddenly soaked my hands and the sheets at the same time as a terrific cramp racked my body. That's when I discovered what it was that my classmates had been boasting about. Suddenly the key was revealed to me for deciphering a previously unknown code. So, the first time I jacked off was involuntary, without forewarning or images. I suppose animals go through something similar when they mate. Stupefied amazement. Definitive proof that even the orgasm is artifice. You never see a young woman walking her dog. What you see is the blond hair blowing in the wind of a damsel straight out of a renaissance painting. You see skinny pants clinging to the interminable legs of a Helmut Newton model. You see the smile resting on Romy Schneider's chin. To observe a fertile human female walking her dog can transcend all physiological aspects and become an epiphany of intolerable beauty. There is nothing crueler than culture. This is Humbert Humbert's tragic realization. Eduardo is a member of the following Facebook groups:

–People who have a scar on their eyebrow.
–People who never eat the cherry on the cake.
–Repentant sluts now happily valley girls.
–People who would prefer to be characters.
–Association of school playground victims.

Likewise, Eduardo "likes":

–Billy bookshelves.
–Schrödinger's cat.
–Expired food.

A waitress in a bar close to where I once worked used to prepare my coffee (black) as soon as I walked through the door, without my having to say a word or make a sign. If I were to go back there after so many years, I wonder if the waitress would still prepare my coffee as soon as I approached the bar. God is familiar with my penchant for writing. God is interested in, and committed to, my career as a writer. God wishes me the best and endeavors to advise me in my work. God says I should write a crime story in which the main character sets out in search of a key object in Western culture, without disdain for religion or non-explicit sex, a clear metaphor (god knows a lot about these things) for unresolved sexual tension. Another possibility is a children's novel, one whose main character, for example, is an adolescent girl threatened by an adult who wants to abuse her while slipping her psychedelic drugs. The girl, aided by her gang of friends (among whom there would be a boy who is deeply in love with her) and a child psychologist from her school, would succeed in confronting the abusive adult. The final scene would consist in the confession and subsequent remorse of the adult in a session that would take place in the psychologist's office, a session that would include the presence of the girl who, moved by compassion, would finally give her attacker a forgiving hug. Sometimes, while going up the stairs of the metro, I have some great ideas. Never going down the stairs. When a student hands an exam to me I think of the symbolic violence contained in that minute gesture. The small act of submission implied by that piece of paper angled downward toward these hands that will subsequently deliver a final verdict. I think that an entire culture is sustained by gestures such as this one. All the great style associated with conquest has been lost. Only from great conquests are great rebellions born. There are times when I think god has gone back to his old ways, that in some way he has recovered his gifts and is capable of entering me through some doorway (there must be a doorway somewhere) and seeing through my eyes and even manipulating my thoughts. For example, when I resolve to start going to bed earlier, when I say no to saturated fats, when I resist having that last drink before getting in my car, or when I look away from the stockings and bouncing skirt of a schoolgirl. I was once stopped by the Spanish Civil Guard at a highway checkpoint. Nervous, I asked one of the policemen, armed with a machine gun, if something was going on. The policeman looked at me indulgently and answered, "When isn't something going on?" Not even someone who had spent twenty years in Tibet, continuously fasting and meditating, could have answered with greater wisdom. María has a cyclamen plant that she waters in the following way: she pours water on a platter and then places the planter on the platter so the roots of the bulb will absorb the water through the orifice beneath. María has baptized her cyclamen with the name, Camilo José Cela. God has so much respect for himself that he addresses himself using the formal *usted*. He says that when he speaks to himself he feels like he's with some extraordinary and other self. I ask him what is so extraordinary about that second person he reveres so much, to which he responds that it is difficult to explain, that I'll have to address my question directly to the other self. Which is impossible because that second person only speaks to god. A singer-songwriter is essentially someone who provides a bath of transcendence to adolescent chaos, a poorly resolved blend of sentimentality and adulterated genius. I can't even listen to Bob Dylan without something churning in my gut. Leonard Cohen and Micah P. Hinson are the exceptions that prove the rule. I've found paper money more often than I've lost it. People tend to see their lives as a succession of events. People are constantly searching for events in novels, in movies, in history books. People are not content to see the price of bread rise, to know that people are living in misery, to see how an infuriated mob takes over a fortress in order to liberate the prisoners. People want to see a bare-breasted woman leading a mob while screaming, "Long live the Revolution!" My life is barren of remarkable events. The women who surround me don't go around bare-breasted waving flags in the air. I like Oriental drawings featuring India ink. There is nothing remarkable in them either. No events. Just beauty and/or the anodyne ugliness of things.

I send more personal (electronic) messages than I receive. I'm not Saint Augustine. I'm not Petrarch. My favorite game is skipping stones. To take a flat stone and send it skimming across the surface of water. To appreciate the erratic succession of bounces and watch as it finally ends by submerging. Writing, this writing, has more in common with skipping stones than with shooting arrows. Consciousness does not precede the very words it uses to refer to itself. I feel neat after clipping my nails. It really bothers me when someone doesn't answer one of my emails. In that case I usually send a second email alluding to my annoyance over their lack of response in a sophisticated and veiled way. If they still don't respond, I send a third and even a fourth email. And so on until my words lay bare the recipient's rudeness. I hardly have any ass at all. However, I have some impressive pectoral muscles. My hair is thick and curly. I'm grateful that my testosterone levels remain low if, in turn, I conserve my mop of hair. I like the Beatles more than the Rolling Stones but less than Joy Division. And yet none of those groups rank above The Doors. The Doors are the guardians of an enigma and a poetry that no musical group has managed to equal. I once crossed the path of a black cat. It took fright, bolted, running and met its end beneath the wheels of a resplendent Mercedes. Its body, still breathing, was writhing on the pavement, its spine broken, like a crazed spinning top. It had bad luck, the black cat. Beauty is a matter of infinitesimals. The slightest nuance marks the difference between the beauty and ugliness of two faces. Between someone and the image of that someone there's a slight detail dictated by the laws of photogenicity. Things that bother me: the noise made by someone eating corn nuts; when someone explodes a balloon next to me; a messy table. My skin adapts easily and quickly to room temperature. God has tried some of my dishes. God thinks I've wasted my talent in the kitchen, that I've made a mistake by not dedicating myself to the culinary profession. I tell him he's wrong, that although I'm more than a good sketcher and a good cook, my only merit is my innate ability for imitation. In fact, I only have talent for words and ideas. One idea can drive me crazy for days or years, unlike an image or a cooking recipe. I'm embarrassed to recall an occasion on which, when I was a teenager, I approached a friend with whom I'd gone to a discotheque. He was whispering into the ear of a girl. I went up to them to ask them if they knew each other. I saw the annoyance in their eyes, the sudden disruption of an enchanted moment. The girl turned around and walked away from us. In that moment, I still didn't understand that seduction is almost always an extraordinary event. That seduction requires a public, but a silent and secondary public. You fall in love when you feel that the whole world around you has become an extra in a movie and that you and your companion are the true protagonists. I believe that we have already lived everything in our dreams, that every night an ungraspable number of images are combined at stellar speeds and that this combination surpasses the number of events in every lifetime. All that we see and feel, all the horrors and delights we have already lived and felt beforehand, although we have forgotten them. I once dreamed that I was already dead and that my life was merely that of a ghost stoically endeavoring to create a dignified biography for a future corpse.

–Plato said that a philosopher should live as if he were dead. In fact, another way that Plato referred to philosophers was as "dead souls."
–Like in Gogol's novel.
–Exactly.
–Someone who buys dead souls, the byproducts of human ism, as a good business.
–A good business?
–Like a self-help book, for example.

By the year 2100 all the people I love will have died. In 1900 none of the people I've loved over the course of my life had been born. I've never understood why adults believe in god and not in, for example, Pérez the Mouse, or The Three Wise Men. When he speaks about the good times he's had, god claims to have been in the mind of famous people like Alexander the Great, Tutankhamun and Napoleon. In fact, he assures me that it was he who communicated to Napoleon the battle techniques used by Alexander and that, two thousand years later, the battle of Austerlitz followed exactly, step by step, the battle of Issus. María sent Eduardo a message including, as usual, an attached photograph along with the following text:

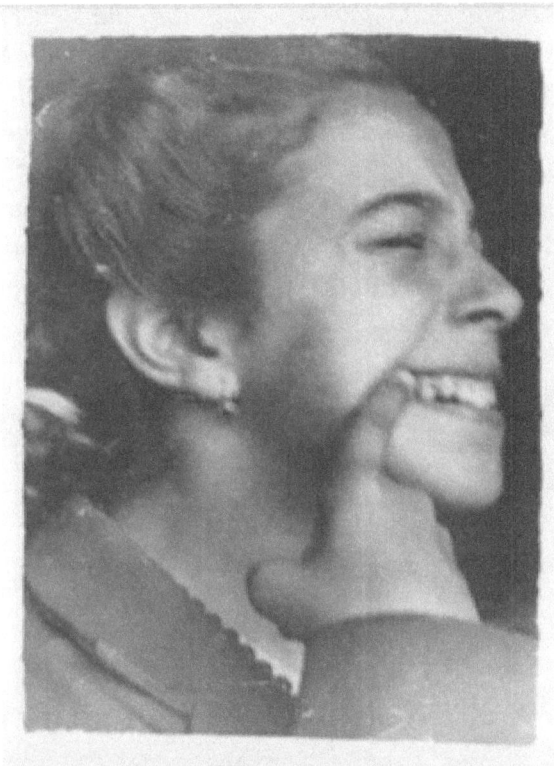

Rosa is seventeen years old and she took this picture of herself. This makes the third of three photographs, followed by one she took at her first communion and another one in which she's with her cousins, Manolita and Paquita (the second generations are always referred to with the diminutive –ita form), at the wedding of her aunt Enriqueta. In the other pictures you can see her face clearly. But this one is different. Her gums were diseased and her teeth jiggled like the keys of

an old organ. The dentist said he would have to pull them. All of the upper teeth. That's why she took this picture before going to the dentist, to be able to see them when she no longer had them. She could cry for her boyfriend who had to go to war (he had to go with the Nationalists but he could have gone with the others, just as the saying goes, "make a friend, make an enemy"), but she prefers to cry for her lost teeth. Although the truth is that she doesn't need to. Her false teeth are terrific. Much better than the real ones. Also, her gums don't hurt anymore. Now Rosa looks at the picture and she thinks it's silly to miss those rotten teeth that wouldn't even let her eat. In fact, she decides not to show it to anyone. Especially not to that boy who comes around to take her out and to whom she revealed her new smile the first time they met in the plaza.

IT TAKES ME APPROXIMATELY TWENTY SECONDS to roll a cigarette. Human babies strike me as being much stranger than the young of any other animal species. When I was a kid I liked to look up the definitions of strange words in the dictionary. I like the sound of bells, but I like even more the song of the muezzin. I've never bet money in a casino. I'd like to conceive of a computer program that would make it possible to somehow measure the distance from one literary work to another. To program a literary measure that computed values between zero and one. The distance, for example, between El Gran Galeoto, by Echegaray, and Finnegan's Wake, by Joyce, would constitute something like the basic unit. I wonder if anyone in this country reads José de Echegaray. María's Facebook profile picture is taken from an issue of the women's magazine, Woman. The picture is of a girl who's so beautiful that none of María's friends would possibly think that it's really María in the photograph, posing in a pretty Halterneck dress, an image that perhaps explains the elevated number of friends that appear listed in her profile and surely explains why at least ninety per cent of the male section viewing the image experience dilation of the corporal ducts capable of transporting aqueous substances. Eduardo's Facebook profile picture is a self-portrait drawn with an Etch-A-Sketch. There are long stretches when María doesn't send any messages to Eduardo. When this happens, Eduardo grows anxious. He's afraid María won't send him any more photographs with her short stories. At times, he wishes he could meet her, but then he remembers that reality is almost always frustrating and that the exceptions to this rule are as improbable as the appearance of a mythological animal. I imagine a work of art consisting in a device that would produce soap bubbles. From a distance of about six or seven feet, standing behind a carnival counter, the spectator would shoot at the bubbles with an air rifle. Mountain climbing seems to me to be a sophisticated way to commit suicide. I fantasize about writing a story called, Confessions of a Pornographer. It would be the story of someone who considers pornography his way of seeing the world, his weltanschauung and his philosophy. In this book, the protagonist would say such things as: the most ancient cosmogony, originating in ancient Egypt, affirms that beings of this world come from drops of semen produced by the god Atum's masturbatory act; pornography is a cultural trap set for human beings just as the orchid is a natural trap for bumblebees, like the grapes painted by Zeuxis for birds to peck at; language is not a virus that uses humans to spread, as Burroughs claimed, but rather images use us to reproduce and multiply; in the beginning it was not the word but rather the image that was in the god Atum's mind at the moment of his orgasm (the primordial image that painters and poets attempt to replicate, an attempt that is doomed to failure); the image of Gorgoneion, with that grotesque mouth and bulging eyes, is none other than the face of the porn actress in Deep Throat; the sexual act is isomorphic to the narrative act; there are as many types of narration as there are acts of masturbation; the sodomite may be recognized for his penchant for metaphor (the substitution of one element for another, of one orifice for another); and whereas the body functions as language in the sexual act, desire activates the complex rhetoric of touching. Felix Salten was the author of Bambi: A Life in the Woods. The very same Felix Salten was also the author of Josefine Mutzenbacher, one of the most scandalous pornographic novels of its time. I imagine a patchwork of the two works, a blend of fragments from Bambi and Josephine. An aliquot blend of sex and sentiment. A perfect work. Sometimes when I'm alone I catch myself in the act of pretending to-be-alone-with-myself. I was born on the 26th day of August. Like Julio Cortázar, like Mother Teresa of Calcutta, like millions and millions of people throughout history. Like just about anyone. Nine months before I was born the Mars 2 space probe crashed onto the surface of Mars. Making telephone calls before twelve o'clock noon on weekends should be prohibited. I've always had a childish face, something that has favored me with the passage of the years. I don't like to read a book all in one sitting. I prefer to switch from one book to another like zapping through television stations. María sometimes flicks through the scanned images in Alma. She stares at them on the screen of her computer and feels a sensation of absence welling up inside of her. When she returns to a normal state of mind it occurs to her that looking at those images is the same as slicing into them in the same way that the knife slices into the eye in those memorable shots in Un Chien Andalou. Then memory emerges, the vitreous humor contained within. She senses that the image that appears on the screen is only the tip of the iceberg of something that is almost always painful. She knows this and yet can't avoid being overcome by shivers provoked by that uncontrollable magma. Photography is a cruel art. All in all, a photograph is a frozen reflection. Melting down those images has the effect of leaving María's eyes brimming with tears. I think that physically beautiful people have less chances of being interesting. Physical beauty implies immediate acceptance. Anyone who is immediately accepted doesn't feel the need to surpass the limits imposed by the threat of non-acceptance; on the contrary, they tend to embrace those limits. The complexity and splendor of a person has to do with overcoming the barriers placed before them by others.

–"God does not reside in healthy bodies," said Hildegard von Bingen.
–You've never made any exceptions?
–Rarely. And only to satisfy my own curiosity.

My facial features are small, almost insignificant. This renders my face a substance that's easy to modify, without particularly distinctive features, almost plastic. A slight grimace can unrecognizably deform the expression of my face. I think of my face as something like a blank page. I believe there's a clear relationship between the human brain and one of those "compressions" by Cesar Baldaccini. I've never known how to choose my own underwear. I lack the taste for it. There is a kind of blindness when it comes to our perception of the other. Communication always involves background noise, blind spots in front of which we erect a set of prejudices and fantasies. I know women who have lived for years with their partner without ever having an orgasm. There are cases in which a woman discovers that her companion is violent, that he is essentially a violent man, which she had been unaware of for as much as ten or fifteen years of living together. I imagine a story in which a top model loses something that is extremely important in her profession: the ability to pose in front of the camera. The photography sessions invariably produce images in which she seems to be blinking or assuming a pose, at times artificial, at times disoriented, in any case always the pose of someone who seems to have suddenly taken off her glasses. Misfortune befalls the model and her professional career. Little by little the jobs start to disappear, fewer and fewer fashion shoots. She loses her luxury apartment, she turns to drugs in order to short circuit the excess of self-consciousness that overcomes her as soon as someone raises a camera in front of her. But the stupor into which she descends thanks to the drugs is not a solution to her problem. Desperate, unable to stop taking drugs, her body begins to lose its treasured natural beauty. Walking down the street, she crosses paths with a cat and longs for the animal's unselfconscious elegance. The cat seems to her to be the quintessential photogenic creature. She wishes, more than anything else in this world, to be like that cat. Which, for a very long time, is exactly how she used to be, but now that has become absolutely impossible. She goes to an expert, a combination of psychiatrist and shaman, an offshoot of the Lacanian school of psychology. He tells her that she only has two possible choices: she can let her life descend into total depravity (panhandlers, the seasoned psychiatrist tells her, possess an uncanny ease and naturality before the camera), or she can set out along an intellectual path entailing studies of the latest advances in mathematics and philosophy. Naturality, the psychiatrist adds, is the exclusive right of beasts and extremely complex beings. The two extremes come together only at the ends of an infinitely long curve. María listens to the psychiatrist but decides not to opt for either of these two extremes. She simply decides to take her image elsewhere, somewhere it will take on another form of beauty, different from that which it has lost. When I was a kid I had a pellet gun. I had excellent aim. I could hit a radio battery at twenty paces. Once I shot a blackbird. I only wounded it. I watched as it fluttered its wings on the ground. My father had to finish it off and put it out of its misery. I took my ball and kicked it against a wall, saying over and over, "I will never shoot another living being." I'd killed some sparrows before, but a blackbird was just too big. I'd never felt so horrible about myself. Sure enough, I've never shot another living being. I'm extremely impatient. On a certain occasion, bored from waiting for them to finish doing my mother's hair, I left her at the beauty parlor, crossed the highway and went home alone. I was four years old. At that same age, I put the canary and its cage into our ultra-capacity washing machine while it was turned on. When my father removed the cage containing the drowned bird, what most surprised me was that the canary still had its intense colors. Eduardo leaves the price tags on everything he's bought from IKEA. The items generally have a group of eight numbers separated by periods. For example, 301.495.56 is the code on the Plastis brush that Eduardo uses to soap his dishes. Eduardo searches the planet for the location that corresponds to the IP for the brush (30.149.55.6 – you have to avoid number combinations that exceed 255). It turns out to be an uninhabited area close to the city of El Dorado in the United States.

Eduardo's mind is then filled with images of Judy Garland entering the magic land of Oz to the tune of Somewhere Over the Rainbow. Next, Eduardo converts the code number of his Plastis soap brush into terrestrial coordinates (30.14 N 95.56 E) and, after entering them into Google Earth, he flies over an area of tea plantations in the Himalayan foothills.

Eduardo not only perceives a certain similarity between the two landscapes but, at this very moment, he realizes there is a steaming cup of green tea on his Jonas desk, a cup that five minutes later he will be washing with his Plastis dishwashing brush. Eduardo feels that the furniture and equipment he bought at IKEA connect him to the world, that through that curious digital analogy, the totality of the universe gathers around him, in the scant four hundred square feet of his apartment. Even someone like Eduardo—someone hardly given to sentimental excesses—feels comforted at seeing how a modicum of poetry has succeeded in injecting some order and sense into the confusion with which he summarizes his life. I've seen some seahorses. I imagine a world in which human beings have disappeared and a parrot perched in a solitary tree recites meaningless words. I feel intense pleasure squeezing through narrow passageways, they fill me with an exciting sense of friction. Proust said that it was thanks to neurotics that most works of art exist, including literary works. Works of art are the product of waking dreams. Like dreams, works of art are emotional simulators, they prepare us for events we have undoubtedly lived through or that we will live through in the future. I write to create an image of future happiness and grief, so that happiness and good fortune don't reduce me to stupidity, so that grief doesn't reduce me to stupor and dysfunction. Perhaps I write so that my future and that of my peers will be less painful. One day I greeted an important publisher with a handshake only a few minutes after masturbating with that same hand. I think I've said that the act of masturbation is very literary. I don't doubt that that publisher had done the same thing a few minutes earlier in his hotel room. With that handshake we confirmed our mutual and definitive love of literature. I don't like to sit at the dinner table if I'm not very hungry. Life is a game of endurance with more or less zero gain. God says that not only life but also World History is a similar game, that he has seen lineages and empires, atop the world for centuries, fall like lead, that good streaks are always balanced by bad streaks because the void and nothingness don't tolerate any lasting competition. Mathematicians call this the "Law of Large Numbers."

–It's the first lesson a broker learns. To buy stocks low and sell them high.
–A principle for making money.
–Precisely. Knowledge that is comparable to that of the Taoist masters. The only sure bet is to bet on the void.

God doesn't dance. Neither do I. God claims that the fact that a man dances is nothing more than another demonstration of the efficacy of the law known as the "Triangle of Desire." God says that only women and gay men like to dance, that gay men dance to display a part of their feminine nature, that gay men get up and dance with women while heterosexual men hang back and watch. Male heterosexuals watch as women let themselves be held in the arms of gay men and are afraid that if they don't respond to this behavior, they'll be excluded from the reproductive cycle. That, and no other, is the reason that heterosexual men imitate the behavior of gays and venture onto the dance floor, plucking up their courage and dealing with the inevitable landslide of ridicule. Frank Sinatra's voice, it seems to me, is as creamy as a cappuccino. I've recorded the sound of the metro entering the station. I've recorded the sound of foam disappearing. I've photographed a chip in the wall the shape of Australia. My first memory could be described as "a boy dressed in a beige suit of short pants running away from a little girl chasing after him. The little boy falls and strikes his eyebrow on a stone." My first memory has to do with an injury. When he speaks, god expresses himself slowly, as if he were addressing a lazy audience who, by some biological miracle, has managed to understand human language. God says that is how you speak when you know what eternity is. Living for eternity has granted god access to a wealth of anthropological laws. The most important of which is that nothing has any meaning. Sometimes I perform acts that lack any apparent meaning. What happens is that when you give it time, you end up assigning your actions meaning that is much more profound than they deserve. The fact that things have no meaning is the perfect excuse for one's imagination to begin to search for their meaning. I remember the first television program I ever watched. Perhaps television leaves some kind of indelible stamp on a person. Perhaps a person's first television program determines their vocation and therefore the future of the person watching. My first television program was Joaquín Calvo Sotelo's *The Bag of Sayings*. In certain light my skin resembles marble. I've never ordered "a bit more than a quarter pound" in any market. I once read somewhere that Nature is obsolete technology. Everything we see happened in the past. Like starlight. I distrust majorities on principle. I don't read what the majority reads. I've never voted for a majority party. It seems obvious to me that the majority is always wrong. The minority is not necessarily any closer to the truth, but lives more freely. I enjoy watching beautiful women, but I enjoy even more observing the face of a man who is staring at a beautiful woman. I think therein lies one of the keys to aesthetics. When I listen to Glenn Gould it occurs to me that the whole world should be able to play the piano in that way. I see Philippe Petit walking a tightrope and I think that anyone should be able to walk a tightrope like that. Mastery of something has the virtue of appearing simple, possible for anyone. Mastery is a kind of supernaturality; the realization of the fantastic. It's as if a chimpanzee, on the basis of aptitude and effort, managed to behave like a human being. Like becoming accustomed to the flight of Superman high above our heads and telling ourselves: "Ah, that's how it's done." There is something inhuman about the way Glenn Gould plays piano and the way Messi dribbles the ball, something that pokes holes in the mattress of predictability on which our humanity comfortably rests. Supernaturality is the void that leaves us speechless, a disquieting *optimus* (a yonder for the species where things may get better, but also where we are taken to the limits of extinction) that very soon becomes *habitus* (the reason for contemplation and real expectations for the rest of the "non-chosen" ones) and which is translated into the messianism of the species. Eduardo's supernaturality consists in his ability to turn his narrow cubicle, filled with objects from IKEA, into an inexhaustible universe. María's supernaturality resides in her complex world of relationships on the internet, in her ability to transform, in real time, every emotion and every feeling into an electronic impulse that she propagates at light speed over the worldwide web. María uses her mouse to catapult her one hundred and twenty-five pounds of weight, converted into pure energy. This transformation of the material into the immaterial is what has always been called the *spirit*. Like so many other beings gifted with supernaturality, both María and Eduardo are perfectly dysfunctional in their conditions as human beings. Walking through the streets or seated in a bar, they both spontaneously incite the same compassion one feels for an animal rejected by its environment. In a right triangle the square of the hypotenuse is equal to the sum of the squares of the lengths of the catheti. Whenever I have to walk between two points I choose the shortest route. In this sense, I suppose I have something in common with the nature of light. Smoking is like a stationary voyage. I was once the singer in a rock group. It was impossible to find a good drummer. That's what my first novel was about. I'm thinking about canned laughter: programming that only uses recordings of canned laughter and, therefore, whenever we hear it we are really hearing the laughter of a whole bunch of dead people. If I were part of a computer I'd be the Random-access memory. When I was fourteen years old my mother made me a flowery vest. I would go out wearing the vest with a gold pocket watch. One time, my father saw me going out dressed like that and called me a faggot. I don't blame him. The word "dandy" wasn't in his vocabulary. *Cavernera*: I know what it means. Sometimes I get on the bus or the suburban train just to eavesdrop on other people's conversations.

–And what do you plan to do next year?
–Register at the university. Since my mother is a professor, I have connections, ha, ha…
–That's good. But register for something cool, okay?
–That's the least of my worries. What I want to do is apply for an Erasmus Grant the year after that. So, I'll register for History, ha, ha…
–History? What are you talking about, man? Register for something that's worth something. Like engineering, for example.
–It doesn't make any difference. All I have to do is pass two courses and I get the Erasmus.
–The way you swing things, man. And your weekend, how was it?
–Great. Saturday we followed my father, me and a couple of friends.
–And how'd it go?
–He was eating with a Minister.
–Which one?
–The Finance Minister. He's a colleague of my father's, ha, ha…
–So why'd you follow them?
–We went into the same restaurant as them and we sat at a table without letting them see us. Later I went over and said hello. As if it was a coincidence. In the end my father

picked up the tab, ha, ha…
–Man, you're too much.
–Ha, ha…

On public transportation, and in many other places, you're faced with an unadulterated reality in a state of stupefying purity. I always get on buses feeling anxious, like a junkie setting out to score some dope. Some people have a penchant for histrionics and outlandish hyperbole. In their presence the most mundane reality can become an uproarious scene from a Spanish zarzuela. God is one of those people. The impetus and motivation of a bodybuilder or an aerobics enthusiast in pursuit of their physical ideal, whatever that may be, undoubtedly surpasses that of an ancient crusader on his quest to reconquer the Holy Land for his true god. When I was a kid I used to like to spy on people through a keyhole. I suspected people of lying, I thought they were all playing a role and that they were only themselves when they were alone. I once closed the living room door where my mother was so that I could watch her through the keyhole. There, standing at her worktable, absorbed in the task of cutting out a sewing pattern, she seemed to be a stranger, someone I didn't recognize. I hardly lasted a minute. I suddenly opened the door and ran toward her. She lifted her eyes from the pattern and, startled, she looked at me for a second before receiving me in her arms. I imagine a film (or perhaps a succession of still shots) that would show everything we miss when we blink our eyes. The images would disappear after a tenth of a second—which is the amount of time a blink tends to last—and then would pass to the next image. Perhaps, by observing this film, a person could discover something essential about their life, some key that would explain things, the secret to our happiness or our fate in life. Once, while walking through the Rastro, I saw a soap bubble floating toward me. It was enormous, the size of a man. I felt the stares of dozens of people turned on me, anticipating how I was going to avoid it. Then, when it was just a few centimeters away from me, I reached out my left hand, slowly and deliberately, Buddhist-like in my lack of premeditation. I felt the drops of soapy water on my skin as the people surrounding me burst into cheers and applause. I've never seen a flying saucer. I once took an exam on religion in school. The teacher, a priest whose balding had spontaneously occurred following the model of the Franciscan tonsure, announced to us that we had all passed the exam, as if arrogating the right to communicate something of divine inspiration. He asked those of us who were not content with a "satisfactory" grade to raise our hands. He told the few of us who raised our hands to stand up. Then he asked who amongst this group wanted a better than "good" grade. Three or four of us raised our hands. He separated us from the rest. He drew very near to us and stared into our eyes as if reading in them the knowledge we had applied while taking the exam. Finally, he asked who amongst this little group would be content with an "excellent." Only two of us refused to raise our hands. The teacher kept his word and gave each of us a grade according to this theatrical and bizarre method. I received a grade of outstanding. I hadn't studied at all for that exam. Among Eduardo's extravagant collection of objects, one that stands out is the hairpiece Santiago Carrillo wore when he returned to Spain from exile and was interrogated by Adolfo Suárez. The wig, a symbol like no other of the Spanish transition, was given to Eduardo by his father. Eduardo's father had been a guard in the detention center of the Director General of Security when Santiago Carrillo was arrested. The personal effects of the communist leader had been left in his care. Knowing that the hairpiece would undoubtedly pass into posterity, Eduardo's father substituted for it the blond, tufted hairpiece of a woman who was a frequent guest of the cells, a woman who exercised her profession in a miserable brothel on Calle Calvario. Thereafter, Eduardo's father kept the hairpiece in safe place and only took it out on special occasions like Christmas Eve and for communions, when his tipsy retelling of the story would raise suspicions of mystification and fraud to be cast on the history of the object. Periodically Eduardo removes the hairpiece from its wax-paper envelope and strokes it as if it were an inherited pet, as if contact with that artificial and fascinating tuft of hair functioned as a time machine that could transport him back through history. Eduardo suspects that the hairpiece symbolizes the Transition and that those disparate men who carried it out could only have reached agreement in some kind of hilarious carnival atmosphere behind closed doors. Only a carnival spirit could have been responsible for an amnesty law that absolved all political crimes committed prior to December 15, 1976, a period extending beyond the Franco dictatorship all the way back to previous centuries, to the Trastámara dynasty, the Recaredos and Leovigildo, to Roman Hispania and, even before that, to Carpetania. Eduardo thinks that this immense farce, called the amnesty, has transformed his country into a place that is free of all guilt with a past that has been transformed into a theme park inhabited by fantasy creatures. Thus, Eduardo was born in the year 4 a. A., that is, *ante* (before) the Amnesty, or before the pardon of all sins. For years I've written in a cubicle below ground level. I like to think that while I'm writing, people are moving about above my head. As if writing had turned me into an anachronistic representative of a cave-dwelling tribe. Writing as an act of primitivism. *La jetée*, by Chris Marker, is a film that summarizes an entire vision of time and, therefore, of existence. A world in which the future is only possible by saving the past, that is, attempting to fill a hole in the past. As if every past instant constituted a kind of worm hole that would enable us to be catapulted into the future. I have slept with many, many more women in my dreams than in reality. The majority of them were women I didn't know. A life is something that doesn't fit into a story. It would be like butchering an elephant and trying to put it in the freezer. One has to chip away at it, to discard pieces, to wonder what it is that one really wants to save. When you look into a glass of milk under the light you can see a cardioid etched on the surface. I once knew a woman who was obsessed by the fact that her right breast was disproportionately larger than her left breast. Closed up in her bedroom she put on a live recording of Silvio Rodriguez performing in the plaza of Las Ventas. A second before the Cuban singer-songwriter sang the line, "*mi unicornio assuul se me ha perdido ayer...,*" I heard the scream of one of his fans. It was her voice that I heard. She was proud of having joined her voice with Silvio Rodriguez's voice there in the plaza of Las Ventas. Then she lifted her shirt and urged me to give her my opinion with respect to the size of her breasts. She was wearing a bra. I didn't know what to say. I didn't see anything abnormal about her breasts. She immediately lunged towards me and gave me a hug and then broke down in a sea of tears. The fascination that girls have with little boxes is a mystery to me. As if, in some way, they knew that they had one inside of them. Reset was a word that the ancient Egyptians used in reference to dreams. The feeling of pertinence is a vestige from the Neolithic period. Whenever it becomes manifest, like the appendix, it is indicative of an infection. The only reasonable solution is to remove it. I lack any feelings of inclusion. In almost all circumstances in life, the situation is the following: I belong, but I am not included. There are parts of me that remain outside of the situation. The fundamental axiom of set theory says that in all sets there exists at least one other set that belongs to it but is not included. I'm one of those sets. Like a rose in a bouquet of flowers. The rose belongs to the bouquet but its "rose-ness" is negligible for the owner of the bouquet. Max Weber said, "Be in the world, but be not of the world. Live in the world as if you did not live in it or form part of it." I prefer listening to people over speaking. In the same way as I prefer reading over writing. Sometimes I let people speak, occasionally agreeing with a nod of my head, my only goal is to know what they think or believe or fear, obedient to an inexplicable anthropological instinct. I can't stand bows on women's clothing, except on their lingerie. There are books that provide ephemeral pleasure, like a kind of intellectual tickling. Other books, however—very few—touch upon select pleasure points, and are like generous lovers who deserve our rapt attention from the first to the last nerve ending. Making love with a pregnant woman is a strange experience. As if someone were watching. Which makes the activity difficult for those of us who don't possess the exhibitionist instinct. In December, 1944, while the baseball player and spy, Moe Berg, was attending a conference given by Heisenberg at the Polytechnic Institute in Zurich (where Einstein formulated his Theory of Relativity a few years earlier), his cousin, Allen Ginsberg, at Columbia University (where five years earlier the first experiment in nuclear fission had been carried out) was meeting the former rugby player, Jack Kerouac. *Piscicola*: I know what it means. Things totally lacking appeal: pan-fried chicken breasts, a clipped toenail on the carpet, a buffet table without a tablecloth, socks hanging on the clothesline, a greasy pan in the sink. The scene of the bone flying through the air in *2001: A Space Odyssey* lasts for exactly seven seconds. Considering that every second consists of twenty-four frames, that makes a total of 168 frames. That's the distance a hominid that has not discovered how to make fire has to travel in order to manufacture a spaceship like the Discovery. If that hominid's launching of the bone were slowed down to coincide with real time (the origin and conclusion of the launch), then each frame would probably last about two or three centuries. I imagine that our present time corresponds to the last frame, just the one in which we can still see the bone but in which the film's audience begins to observe the splendor of the spaceship plowing through the darkness of space. That frame encapsulates all of us, that bone, rising into the air and finally becoming the most perfect metaphor of all time. The centuries attributed to this image have been glorious centuries, brimming with great works of art and new discoveries. However, humanity is still represented by a bone, a metaphor loaded with primitive connotations which will inevitably change beyond the culminating frame. End of ellipsis. Turning point. This narration cannot surpass such a limit. In this world of the Discovery Space Shuttle there is no place for a book like this one. *2001* is one of the few perfect films because (among other reasons) no one reads anymore and because in none of the scenes of the film does a book actually appear, not even a closed book.

–It's 28590
–What are you talking about?
–The last frame in which the bone appears.
–It could be any frame.
–Of course, but it's that one, precisely that one. Columbus could have discovered America in a different year, but it was 1492. Also, 28591 is a prime number.
–Which is the first frame in which the space ship appears.
–That's right.
–Which means…
–That it can be used as a unit of measurement. That it can't be divided into equal parts. That it's incommensurate with all the frames that precede it.
–Great. Do you think Kubrick was aware of that?
–I don't suppose so.
–I suppose it doesn't matter.
–I wouldn't say that. Also…
–Yes?
–If we enter 28590 in Google Maps…

–…
–We come to Mecca.
–Another monolith?
–Another monolith.
–Fantastic. Everything has meaning.
–Nothing has meaning. Remember that.
–But it could have meaning.
–With this material we could write a fantastic story.
–I don't know. It's not very credible.
–But it's reality.
–That's what I mean.

I once dreamed that the president of the United States (Obama) kidnapped our president (José Luis Rodríguez Zapatero). Following the initial moments of confusion, life went on as usual with the citizens resigned to the kidnapping. This dream can be interpreted in at least two ways; one of them—it seems to me—is pretty obvious. In the afternoon light I've seen the reflection of a naked woman in the glass door of a terrace. María likes to browse through a family album in which there are pictures of her as a little girl and as a teenager. Her poses are always elegant. If she ever appears in a photograph with anyone else it's María who stands out, like a black hole absorbing all the light, scarcely sharing any with the other bodies. María, until the age of twenty-two, had been the spoiled child of all cameras. *Denton*: I know what it means. I saw a teenage girl brushing a dog as white as her own dress beneath the midday sun on a Mediterranean beach. Underwater, while scuba diving over a colony of posidonia, I remember reciting the periodic table of elements. María worked for several years as a photographic model. She didn't dominate magazine covers, but her face was common in fashion and related publicity campaigns. Everything was going well until the day that, while walking down the street, she felt something drop to the ground. She stopped and, spinning around, looked for the wayward object. It was her lighter. She didn't know how it could have fallen out of her handbag. She bent down to retrieve it and, straightening back up, she saw in front of her one of those billboards that covers the sides of buses. It was an image of Kate Moss. María realized that her own posture at that moment was the same as the model's. With one foot forward and her torso slightly tilted, Kate Moss was holding a bottle of perfume, whereas she was holding her lighter. By way of her reflection in the advertisement María became aware of how unnatural her own stance was. She stood up straight, put her lighter in her bag and walked away, feeling almost embarrassed. From that moment forward, she was conscious of her strange way of walking. Something struck her as disagreeable in the exaggerated way she swung her legs, as if she were trying in some absurd way to trip over herself. She tried to widen her stride. As she walked she examined her reflection in the store windows and she could hardly recognize herself. At the next modeling session something wasn't working. The photographer cleaned the lens. He changed the filter. He substituted one camera for another. Nothing helped eliminate the blurriness of María's image as if someone had rubbed their finger over the image still damp with ink. If she didn't project a nervous smile, then she forced an inexpressive grin onto her face that was more the grimace of a hieroglyphic than of a young woman proud of her beauty. You look like you want to take a shit. You have the face of someone who just took an enormous stinking dump and who can't find the toilet paper, said Darío, her lover, and the photographer of the agency she worked for, who was now upset over this repeated and unfathomable failure. Suddenly, María seemed to have lost her mysterious photogenic gift. The casino in Murcia: where Ortega y Gasset met his future wife, Rosa Spottorno, and where years later Miguel Espinosa suffered a heart attack that would land him in his grave. God claims that he inhabited Walter

Benjamin's mind before he blew his brains out in a hotel in Port Bou. An instant before pulling the trigger, god goes on to tell me, he had an absolutely brilliant idea in his mind and he fantasized that, as if the thought had crystalized into a kind of diamantine image, the thought would render the bullet incapable of passing through but rather would ricochet and exit his head. When I ask him what the idea was, god winks at me and says that now he is the only one who knows Walter Benjamin's last idea (except, perhaps, for Charlie Kaufman, the screenwriter of *Being John Malkovich*), an idea the German managed to name in the final moment before detonation: Überlebenbildenwissenschaft. "The science of the survival of images," god translates extemporaneously. God is completely unable to explain how Charlie Kaufman could have gotten hold of Walter Benjamin's last idea unless god isn't the only one to possess this gift of being able to invade the consciousness of others. Perhaps, on some future occasion, he could share with Kaufman the consciousness of another human being; or, he now fantasizes, he could even visit the mind of this much-admired screenwriter. The imagination does what the body cannot, and the body can do nothing if it hasn't been imagined first. There are times when María is practically convinced that she should get to know Eduardo *personally*. She knows that a message to his inbox in which, rather than a photograph and a story, the text would say something like, *Hi, my name is María and...* would be enough to start a *relationship*. But María, who for a long time has lost her self-image to the point of not recognizing herself in any photograph, knows that the María who would emerge in this message is a María who has completely disappeared and that the real María is the one that now travels over the net at the speed of light, materializing on the screen via her Facebook profile and her image-story combinations. Eduardo surprises himself at times, crouched over his can of stewed beans like an animal wary of other animals that might try to steal his prey. In those moments he sits up, aware of the absurdity of the idea that someone in this house, which is absolutely empty, might contend with him for his expired can of beans. On a certain occasion, I experienced an emotion that arose from a personal situation, which metamorphosed into the opposite emotion and then this emotion, in turn, was transformed back into the original emotion. All this I analyzed under the lens of an altered consciousness, thanks to the ingestion of drugs. I learned that the self installs itself in the identification and fixation of that movement that expands in a continuous manner between two opposites. I don't believe in any kind of purity. To create poetry is to throw out bait for time and wait for something to bite. Words, I mean. Things that take me back to my childhood: the smell of suntan lotion; in winter, a scarf that smothers your face; a vinyl sofa; a Rubio handwriting notebook; a black-and-white television; the sensation of boredom. *Bergamot*: I know what it means. Here is another image that María sent to Eduardo, with its companion story:

IN THIS IMAGE YOU SEE *a scene on Cape Palos. A shot of two officials in the Italian navy. One of them, on the right, is Captain Piccone. It's August 4, 1906 and the transatlantic ocean liner, the SS Sirio, has just sunk, having struck the rocks off the Hormigas Islands. The true dimensions of the disaster are still unknown. From the pocket of Captain Piccone's jacket a book protrudes, the only possession he managed to save from the shipwreck. It's a translation into Italian of the novel, The Unknown, by Benito Pérez Galdós. Since he left port in Genoa, reading The Unknown has been one of Captain Piccone's few pleasures on what will be his last mission before retirement. Over the course of the voyage he let his second-in-command take the helm on several occasions while he took refuge in his cabin to become absorbed in his reading of The Unknown. He would open the book and dive into the pages, which crashed one by one upon his consciousness like waves upon the seemingly solid hull of the ship. As he was turning one of those pages he heard the terrible crunch. He lifted himself from the floor and picked the book up from the carpet before leaving his cabin.*

Very few things happen in The Unknown. *In fact, the plot is quite banal. Through a series of letters, the protagonist tells us of unrequited love and the death of a friend. The narrator doesn't understand why he's been rejected by the woman he loves; he doesn't know if his friend was murdered or whether, perhaps, he committed suicide. In* The Unknown *there are such lines as:*

...and what exasperating monotony in the whole of life; what boredom in this immense jungle of laws, which prevent our slightest movement; what immense tedium in this system that complicates all things, to kill the unknown, the unknown, Manolo my very core, the unknown, the joy of souls, the salt of existence!...

Lines that sounded enigmatic to the ears of Captain Piccone, and at the same time that spoke to him directly in a part of himself that he couldn't place with certainty. Captain Piccone didn't understand how one could construct a plot based on nothing. He was amazed that the recipient of the letters was named X. He imagined himself as Mr. X, that the letters were addressed to him. Piccone, for the first time in his life, enjoyed imagining himself as an unknown person.

I LOVE SINKING MY TEETH into hardened toothpaste and feeling the way it melts in my mouth as it makes contact with my saliva. I almost never remember how a book ends. *PAPP-A blood test*: I know what it means. Bench press: 132 pounds. Deltoids lateral raise: 22 pounds. Biceps curl: 55 pounds. Dorsal raise: 110 pounds. Anaerobic exercise: 15 minutes. Millimeter by millimeter, year after year, I'm slowly reducing the circumference of my abdomen. Who knows, perhaps I'll stop writing soon. I've made little boats out of bamboo leaves and thrown them into the water of a ditch. Two or three times in my life I've been confused with someone else in the street. One of those times was in France. Whenever I wash leeks, I rub one against another under a stream of water. I love the harsh feeling of that rubbing action. Everything is fragmented. Everything is interrelated. María looks at photographs from her childhood and adolescence and hardly recognizes herself. She admires the features of that beautiful girl, unable to know what she is feeling. She believes that the only way to approach that unrecognizable vestige of the past is through a story, that only through fiction can she possibly figure out who that adolescent was posing in the park at Retiro with the composure of a feline surprised in the midst of the jungle. In 1916, Tristan Tzara and Vladimir Ilyich Ulyanov (better known as Lenin) often meet at the Cabaret Voltaire. They play chess (Lenin invariably chooses to be black). Lenin likes Tristan's last name, a name that reminds him of his arch enemy: the Tsar of all of Russia. It reminds him that he has a mission in life. Lenin feels uncommon pleasure in declaring checkmate and, following the resigned assent on the part of his opponent, toppling the king (invariably white) with a sharp blow to the crown. Tzara likes to hear Lenin's shouts during one of his drinking rampages. That repeated *da-da* as he waves an arm to the rhythm of the music in the Cabaret Voltaire. During the chess game, Tzara frequently makes arbitrary moves, lacking all logic, as if he were likening himself to a force of nature, which infuriates Lenin, whose moves are guided by an implacable logic, faithful to the dictates of materialism. The white king, the Tsar, is an object that can be known. His nature, however, is elusive. The player of the black pieces, exemplary revolutionary subject that he is, closes in on the object of his quest for knowledge, the Tsar. This knowledge allows for two predicates: obliviousness and an intimate desire for annihilation. Every time he topples his adversary's king, Lenin feels that he's carrying out the only possible synthesis of the two predicates. I went to three elementary schools and two high schools. When I was in the eighth grade a classmate waited for me outside of class in order to bully me with insults and shoves. I didn't defend myself. He followed me and called me a son of a bitch. I hadn't done anything to deserve this harassment. I was new at the school. I didn't know anyone who I could turn to as a friend. That kid hated me for no reason. Increasingly pissed off, he demanded to know why I didn't do anything when he called me a son of a bitch. I told him it was for the simple reason that my mother wasn't a bitch. Daniel Caballero Molina was his name. He taught me that hatred is banal and inexplicable, like all the other forces of nature. Not long ago I received a friend request on Facebook in his name. Naturally, I accepted. Every so often Eduardo takes time to look at apartments on www.idealista.com. He browses apartments of three and four bedrooms, with polished parquet floors, of more than thirteen hundred square feet. Luxurious apartments of absolutely unattainable charm. That's when he's beset by a boundless nostalgia, a feeling, he imagines, like the one under whose influence poets sit down to write their masterworks. I never learned to blow smoke rings. When I was a teenager I had great artistic ability. Now, however, to sit in front of a piece of paper or a canvas with a brush in my hand is an unimaginable fantasy. I've danced naked under the light of the moon staring at an awakening city that appeared to me in that moment to be an ovule whose fertilization

I would have been willing to fight for. María now works in a wig boutique in the center of Madrid, in the Lavapiés neighborhood. She opened the business with the savings she'd put away during the days she worked as a fashion model. She has no special calling for this business. It was more of a default decision. She discovered that after she'd eliminated all the other imaginable possibilities for her future, her mind kept returning to the image of a wig, no wig in particular but rather an abstract wig, the wig in and of itself, a noumenon wig. On one of the expeditions outside his home, which Eduardo feels compelled to do occasionally to restock his supply of canned bean stew, he discovers a sign at the entrance to the San Andrés church on which a panhandler has written:

> If your <u>Key</u> be true
> I'm o<u>Kay</u> to stay with you
> KiKe

Which brings to mind, for Eduardo, Saussure's theory of the hypogram whereby the theme of the tiny poem is perhaps the subjectivity of Enrique himself, a man without family, isolated from the normal modes of urban communication and representation. I can't stand drafts in a house, not even in the summertime. They give me goose bumps, they irritate me. Eduardo suffers from occasional epileptic seizures. Over the course of time he's managed, if not to prevent them, to anticipate them through a series of indicators that function like proleptic elements in a scene from a made-for-TV horror film. All of a sudden, his perception of the world will begin to break up, to be perforated by increasingly frequent lapses, like a film from which a censor has clipped out frames at random, or like a landscape reconstructed from a long train ride periodically interrupted by tunnels. As a palliative during these seizures, Eduardo uses a bone he bought at a pet shop, a bone like the one the simian throws into the air in *2001: A Space Odyssey*, a bone that, if the symptoms of the crisis don't interfere, Eduardo uses to avoid swallowing his own tongue. One of those seizures caught him unprepared while sitting on his Karlstad couch, watching television. He groped on the table and all around him, seeking the bone to no avail. The crisis was imminent. The program Eduardo was watching at that moment, a reality show, had transitioned into a kind of photomontage directed by Dziga Vertov that was intended to show a sightseeing tour of the most lurid spots of emotional decrepitude. The emergency solution consisted in grabbing the remote control and biting down hard on it between his teeth. At the height of the crisis, with his teeth chattering, the channels erratically flickered by before Eduardo's vacant gaze: Duran i Lleida threatened to withdraw his support from the Government if the inalienable rights of Catalonia weren't recognized; a girl asked an invisible audience to name the capital of France (five letters); Ángel Gabilondo was interviewing the Basque regional president; Juan Manuel de Prada was speaking about the inalienable rights of the unborn child; a member of the People's Party, whose last name was the same as one of Franco's ministers, regretted the statements of Duran i Lleida, but even more the Government's passive attitude; a muscular man with bigorexia, perched on a platform, pulled ropes on pulleys while smiling into the camera; and, lastly, at the same slow-motion pace as Eduardo began to regain consciousness, a bone rising and rising into the air and finally turning into a spaceship plowing through outer space. The first thing Eduardo sees when he regains full consciousness is that spaceship. Precisely frame 28591 of *2001: A Space Odyssey*. God annoys me. I tell him he annoys me and he tells me that it's all part of a deliberate strategy to avoid the stagnation of my evolutionary process. God says that without external and internal irritations every being tends toward self-similarity. As examples he cites trees, seashells, snails, cauliflower... I should thank him. Only an irritating environment avoids this elemental morphogenesis that makes the whole into the image and likeness of its parts. He goes on to tell me that the history of humanity follows this same scheme. That Napoleon is only a likeness of Alexander the Great and that the Gulf War follows in the footsteps of the Trojan War.

–And Helen of Troy?
–The weapons of mass destruction.
–The weapons that never turned up.
–Helen didn't either. I told Herodotus.
–And the end of the story?
–A traditional gnostic myth.
–Francis Fukuyama is a gnostic?
–No doubt about it. Have you heard about the Project for a New American Century?
–No.
–It's god's realm on earth incarnated by North American civilization.
–Do you think they have a future?
–None. War is the mother of all things.
–That's from Heraclitus.
–I don't deny it. I was in his head when he thought of the aphorism.
–You? In his consciousness?
–That's what I mean.
–Whoever speaks of war speaks of irritation.
–It's the same thing.
–Is there any other case of that morphogenetic law?
–There's thousands of them.
–I'm not asking for that many.
–The Faustian bargain.

–Faust was an imaginary character.

–Depending on how you look at it. There are documented cases of deals with the devil.

–Let's cut to the chase.

–Tinkerbell, Paris Hilton's Chihuahua.

–Really?

–He's the devil. Paris Hilton is our modern-day Faust.

–Paris Hilton sold her soul to the devil in exchange for her happiness.

–Exactly.

–So, she'll die when she's satisfied.

–I'm not so sure about that.

–What do you mean?

–I'm not so sure about complete satisfaction. Paris Hilton can't get absolute satisfaction. Indulgence is an infinite realm that knows no end.

–How do you know so much about Paris?

–I was inside her.

–Just like the others.

–You said it.

–You're the one who should write a book.

–I don't write. It's an ancient custom.

–Getting back to Paris…

–The devil will get tired.

–Tinkerbell.

–Yes.

–And will abandon her.

–It's likely. The devil gets tired of banality because everything about him has to do with banality. He wants to differentiate between good and evil. So, he needs the souls of others.

–Like a playwright.

–Something like that. But on a universal scale.
–And he'll return to his usual form somewhere in Beverly Hills. What is his usual form?
–I have no idea.
–I guess you've never been inside of him.
–Impossible.
–Why?
–Because he was expelled for having looked. He was expelled for looking inside of god. He watches god.
–Like in Kaufman's film.
–Exactly.
–Maybe Kaufman is the devil. Maybe Kaufman is inside of you now.
–Dictating all of this to me.
–Could be. Kaufman always seemed confused to me.
–Am I being confusing?
–Very.

Things that I think are pleasant: the shadow of a stonewall on a summer day; the image of light beams when I open my eyes underwater; crossing a bridge over a river in a light rain. There are two kinds of people, those that see the world with a prejudice that they find confirmed everywhere, and those that have a prejudice and the values to see the world without preconceptions. I don't like people who immediately form a neat idea of things, who know with certainty how other people are and, therefore, feel empowered to judge them. Things (and especially people) don't have an absolute image. When I was a kid I could see from my house in La Cueva a building on a hill. In some ways, that building was inaccessible, although I could have reached its doors by taking a long hike. I used to imagine that it might be a school, or a penitentiary, or a secret military installation… I never asked anybody about it. I never even thought about going there. I settled for fantasizing about its existence from a distance. Anyone who believes in eternal life can't be trusted. Belief in an absurdity that lies beyond all possibility discredits any human being. In such a person's presence we should protect ourselves the way we would against a dangerous criminal. With god it's different. Eternal life... It's exhausting just to think about it. I have a confusing memory from when I was four years old. While bouncing my ball in the courtyard I felt someone watching me. From the neighbor's terrace the owner of the house was staring at me. Her son, a few years older than me, had died several days before from a brain tumor. The woman watched me for a long time. It wasn't a sad stare, but rather she seemed irritated. I was frightened and ran into the house to hide. Men tend to have erotic dreams with anonymous women while women have them with specific men. Men love the genotype. Women love the phenotype. Men tend toward abstraction. Women, toward detail. For Eduardo the meanings of such words as *enthusiasm* and *ambition* are like those variables that form part of an equation whose solution we know exists but that, even so, we can't grasp. Children are the masters of eternal recurrence. I ask god to be more explicit about what he means by Überlebenbildenwissenschaft, "The-science-of-the-survival-of-images." He kindly explains to me that the best way to get a clear idea of what Überlebenbildenwissenschaft consists in is to imagine one set in relation to another set that is different from the former. The new set of relations shall be potentially infinite. Überlebenbildenwissenschaft basically consists in the art of selection within the infinite possibilities presented by this new set.

–Could you give me an example?
–World history and the placement of products in a supermarket. Organ meats, for example, are always at the back (I'm not quite sure I get the idea of what god is trying to tell

me. God seems to notice my confusion.)

–Or, real-function variables and states of consciousness.

–…

–Let's take the equation, $x^2 = x+1$, where one of the solutions is the golden ratio. And let's consider the basic act through which the subject gains consciousness of itself, an act that we can illustrate in the following way: $I - I = I + Id$. Or, alternatively, $I^2 = I + id$.

–Or, as introspection leaves one by oneself accompanied only by the fiction of identity.

–There you go, you learn fast.

I've repeatedly studied myself. Yet I've never discovered anything. I've only learned things about what's there outside of myself. My thoughts form part of the landscape. Sometimes Eduardo calls the numbers of the owners of those unattainable apartments listed on the website, www.idealista.com. He pretends to be a caller interested in seeing an apartment with the intention of renting or buying, depending on the situation. It's a cheap kind of entertainment that enables him to visit homes that he would never have entered otherwise. Eduardo derives immense pleasure from visiting those beautiful homes whose proprietors he doesn't even know. He chooses the layout that most appeals to him and asks the agent to leave him alone for a minute so he can consider the convenience of the potential future home. During that time Eduardo admires the objects and furnishings and takes pleasure in imagining that he is the legitimate owner of all those belongings. But he takes even greater pleasure in abandoning those things when, after waving goodbye, he goes out the door knowing that he has enjoyed the delights of that home without having suffered any of its inconveniences, like a satisfied lover furtively slipping from a woman's bed after indulging the cravings of the flesh with the knowledge that he'll never see her again in his entire life. I like using a new toothbrush for the first time. When I was a kid I would fantasize about being a Roman legionnaire. I suppose what attracted me about legionnaires was the blend of a suggestive aesthetic and the quest for unexplored lands. I derive immoderate pleasure from discovering things that nobody seems to have discovered before. A stain on the wall in the shape of the map of Australia. A champagne nuance in the odor of damp earth. I've taken LSD. I've smoked marihuana. I've taken ecstasy and psilocybin. I've never taken peyote. I prefer ceramic knives to those of steel. The degree of a culture's evolution and refinement is demonstrated by the utensils it uses for cutting: they are an obvious metonym for its analytical ability. That's why, in my view, Japanese culture is superior to others which entrust the cutting of objects to corrodible steel blades. There was a time in her life when María saw herself as a broken toy that would never again perform the functions for which it was conceived, specifically one of those ragdolls that someone has emptied of its stuffing. This occurred during the period when she was taking aggressive medication as prescribed by her psychiatrists. It was during that period of her life that María came to the conclusion that she was empty. Really, she didn't feel anything. It was this total lack of feeling that finally led her to think that she was no different from a doll on a shelf. That was when she took a box cutter and sliced her skin from armpit to ankle, just as if she were an envelope. She wanted to see if she contained a message inside. That's how she got the scar she rubs occasionally. It was her first step. She discovered, to her surprise and at the same time with a celebratory spirit, that there was a body made of fat and muscle beneath the surface of her skin, a body that bled and desired to hold onto life. She slashed her own image. Her face didn't shudder from the predictable gust of air that escaped from the void but rather from the alarming odor of her own blood. The doctors were baffled by María's convalescent smile. They didn't understand the consolation she derived from her awareness of her own capillaries and entrails, much less the almost fetishistic admiration she held for that crease that converted the reflection of her beautiful body in the mirror into an artistic and utterly desirable imitation of the empty set. Wittgenstein and Adolf Hitler were classmates at the *Realshule* of Linz. I don't know if they ever spoke to each other (it's certainly possible). In any case, I imagine that any communication between them couldn't have been any more fluid than that of a Neanderthal and a Homo Sapiens trapped together in a cave during a storm. I have a hard time remembering birthdays. I'm surprised at the way adults have difficulty hearing elderly people when they speak, simply assenting or interspersing periodic questions to simulate interest while they do other things. I think some works of art are better than their makers and that's why they endure. Like those seashells that make us forget the creatures they once sheltered. One summer afternoon on Syros I quarreled with the woman I was traveling with. We spontaneously separated. Neither of us knew the city. I walked aimlessly for hours through the labyrinth of streets that made up the ancient city, built on the side of a hill. I came to a scenic lookout. From there, contrasted with the darkness of the night, I could see the lights of the ferries that were moving about in the harbor. It was then that I felt a presence at my side. I turned. It was my companion. She came toward me. We embraced without speaking a word. Eduardo is often assailed by childhood memories, memories that almost always have to do with his father. It's not that Eduardo was orphaned from his mother or that he didn't have friends or memorable experiences, but rather that his father occupies a central spot in his memory, like the sun around which all other memories orbit. He remembers, for example, when, at the age of seven, after one of the ping-pong matches they invariably played on Saturday afternoons in the playroom, his father put a ping-pong ball in his hand and squatted down so as to bring his unshaven face close to Eduardo's, and said:

–Keep this ball, son, take it in your hands, accustom yourself to its feel, learn from its emptiness. You should know that this ball is much more than the 2.7 grams of celluloid that give it form; what's important are the cubic centimeters of nothingness it holds inside. 33.5 cubic centimeters of nothingness. The age of our lord, Jesus Christ, my son. It's the void that makes beings into something fantastic. We all have something of that void inside of us, but no being is as exceptional as the sphere, as this sphere. A semi-transparent surface closed over a vacuum. The most similar thing to a soap bubble. Do you remember how much you used to like playing with soap bubbles? That's why the sphere is the perfect metaphor, like the seed of all metaphors, because the void is what enables us to put things in relation to other things, because we all carry in side of us something of that void. We are all brothers in the void. When we go to the supermarket and we pass by the chocolates, in spite of your stamping and screaming and your tears that get you nowhere. Analyze that moment, son, think about it. That is the void. Numbers are based on the void. Power, whatever people may think, is an empty place. Increasingly empty. And Sundays, son, have you ever thought about Sundays? Sunday is the void of the week. There will come a day, son, when many people will miss *el Generalísimo*, because *el Generalísimo* was a presence, although he could easily be confused with the void. And that's the secret of the Civil Guard, a doctrine that can only be passed on to the initiated, and you're one of them now. You're one of us, son. Look at the tricorn hat. Do you see? No, not like that, look at it from the side. Tell me what you see. (To Eduardo it seemed that the tricorn took on the form of one of those spaceships that appeared on after-din ner-sci-fi-TV movies.) Yes, I see, you're so amazed you don't know what to say. You've guessed it. You've always been a bright kid. It's the shape of the empty set. A crossed-out circle. I've seen how you've drawn it with your Etch-A-Sketch, over and over. You'll be lucky, son, I can see that your future will be overflowing with the void, wherever you look you'll find the most amazing of all voids. My boy, you don't know how much I envy you. And of all the balls, none is like the ping-pong ball. Forget the soccer ball, tennis balls... The ping-pong ball is the only one made of celluloid, the same material as movies are made from, did you know that? The ping-pong ball is mysterious. If you follow the flight of the ball in the air over the table, it's like watching a movie, a movie projected by a unique camera, unrepeatable, fantastic. And it's always a movie about the void, about the secret of the world; and every stroke with the paddle is an unexpected twist, a little catastrophe, a way of advancing the movie toward its liberating end. Like when those soap bubbles exploded. Do you hear me? Are you listening, son?

Every day Eduardo does a Google search for the word "love" and among the results he chooses one new entry. He's still far from knowing its meaning. Whenever the date of my birthday approaches I feel the need to begin a new book, or to give a boost to the one I'm currently writing. *It is like all...* A phrase that always amazes me. A phrase that represents the ultimate expression of poetic laziness. Eduardo has the pale blue eyes of a fighter pilot, a gaze that only becomes expressive and human after achieving remote and improbable objectives at supersonic speeds. I can't understand why, despite putting my clothes into the washer right side out, when I remove them, they're always reversed. There's an objective, chthonic and sexual component to the way female hockey players rest the ends of their hockey sticks against their *mons ven-*

eris at the same time as they raise their left hands to their breasts, with rapt faces, listening to strains of the national anthem. Once a week Eduardo sweeps his apartment and passes a dust cloth over the lacquered surfaces of his IKEA furniture. When his surroundings have reached an acceptable level of cleanliness, he returns to his Allak model armchair, he opens an online window of contacts on his Facebook profile page and thinks of the Italian Franciscan monk, Joaquin de Fiore, and his prophecy about the Age of the Holy Ghost, an age in which humanity would only consist of perfect monks who would relate to each other without the intervention of any human authority. Or sexual authority, it should be added. In the Age of the Holy Ghost sex is beside the point. The speed at which the sexual act takes place is abnormally low, to which should be added the complications inherent to any type of unplugged and analog relationship. "Too much effort for too few rewards" could be the phrase that summarizes the complex philosophy that drives the issue. Eduardo likes to draw. But he doesn't use color pencils or brushes, but rather an Etch-A-Sketch that he has kept with him since childhood. Eduardo has risen to such a level of mastery that within minutes he is able to sketch any imaginable figure, including faces and landscapes. His favorite subject is the self-portrait. Sitting before the bathroom mirror, under the lighting of the Basiks brand wall lights, he draws his reflection as faithfully as possible. When he's finished, he shakes the Etch-A-Sketch until the image has completely disappeared. Over time he's come to realize that the last thing to disappear on the screen is the scar over his right eyebrow, something for which he has not yet found a satisfactory explanation. I imagine the following situation: in the drawer of a dresser a boy finds a film. The film, whose title seems to be a date, is hidden under the wedding dress of his mother. The boy waits for his parents to go out before watching it. On the television he watches his parents in their bedroom, he watches them undress and get into bed. They mate savagely, in a way the boy would never have imagined possible for his dad and mom. In the film, the boy no longer sees his dad and mom. Instead, he observes a young and healthy couple, a pair of exemplary members of the species who carry out the reproductive act with great passion. This filial oblivion leads to the boy's having an erection. The boy's excitation precludes any prejudice linked to kinship and the boy reaches orgasm simultaneously with the couple on the television. When he's finished, the boy removes the tape from the player and looks again at the date on the title. He discovers that the date is nine months prior to the date of his own birth. Things that arouse a feeling of melancholy: a Sunday afternoon, a music band in a town we're passing through, a birthday cake. "I don't know myself in both ways, neither in body or soul, and I see myself as nothing." This is a sentence that María read in a work by Hildegard von Bingen and that she intimately associated with her state of mind during a period of her life. I decide to take advantage of my friendship with god to ask him for a favor. I dare him to enter the consciousness of someone of my choosing. At first god refuses. He says he has never entered the consciousness of anyone at someone else's request. Later he says that he's willing to do it if it has to do with something important. I remain silent. Finally, he says he'll do it, flat out. So I tell him that I want him to enter the mind of Enrique, the beggar who lives in the doorway to San Andrés church. I was the singer for a musical group. The group was called *La tragedia*. It was a rock band dedicated to the metaphysical scream. In a certain way, I believe I've always aspired to stop being a specific person in order to become something else. To enjoy several lives over the course of one life. Like a kind of humble game of reincarnations. Like giving life to an unknown. I'd like to become a writer writing his final work. In this final work the writer declares that he will stop writing. The work, which would paradoxically address the act of renouncing writing, would become a theory and a practice of this very same renunciation. In this work the writer would exclusively speak the truth. The truth is almost always disgusting. We are capable of inventing anything in order to hide the truth. Toilet paper and literature. One writes in order to tell lies, in order to transform real situations through fiction or simply to lose oneself in fantasy. A work that deals with the truth and tells the truth can't be a literary work. In such a work, the writer would reveal his disdain for literature, an activity he would voluntarily renounce, considering it vacuous, superfluous, outdated. Plot is a forensic leftover, an inheritance of discourse with which the assassin would attempt to exonerate himself or with which the jury would seek to condemn the alleged perpetrator. In the story of a crime, dissected by a jury, there is guilt and, at the same time, redemption. Over the course of his trial, the dissecting of clues and motives, the accused finds justification for his crime, he tells himself that this is its meaning. Discard plot. Defend innocence.

–Judge and you shall be judged.
–I pass. I'm innocent.

You kill in order to know yourself, so that someone will tell your story. To save yourself. María's interrupted career was a blow for the modeling agency that employed her. The agency had entertained high hopes for her professional future. Having received evidence (photographs taken by professional photographers employed by the agency itself) of María's sudden lack of photogenicity, the agency made the decision to put together a report that would reveal María's extraordinary case to the world. The photographs for the article show a nebulous María, as if her facial muscles had broken ranks and fled in disarray. Her expression is one of total disorientation, of a defenseless animal startled in its nest by an explosive flash. The article focuses on the fact that one of the most beautiful women in the country had suddenly become completely unfit for posing before the camera. It wasn't that María betrayed the lens, but rather that the glare of the lights was absorbed by her skin, by every orifice of her body, like that of a Danae who submitted pleasurably to the desires of a divinity, at the same time as every cell seemed to resist that same light as if she were defending herself against an attacking rapist. The writer of the article went further, daring to offer an explanation: an acute case of physiological instability due to hyperthyroidism or hypoglycemia. Or else… an even stranger case of hypersensitivity to the light of the flash resulting in photophobia perhaps due to—still undiagnosed—Chiari malformation (for obvious reasons, albinism was ruled out). In a maneuver of theoretical brilliance, the journalist compared María to one of the figures painted by Leonardo da Vinci, figures that seem to have been trapped mid-movement by the renaissance master's pencil. Leonardo himself stated that objects (and therefore people also) were spinning, even though they appeared to be stationary, and this spinning motion was a manifestation of the soul contained in all bodies. Therefore, the writer concludes, not without a certain ironic tone, María could consider herself fortunate as she had lost her photogenicity but, in exchange, she had gained something more important: a soul. Because of this article, María decided to create a new folder in her computer, a folder she didn't hesitate to call Alma. The first things María saved in Alma were the photographs that had appeared in the article. Leonardo was right. In all things there is a tendency toward movement. For this reason, particles become waves. For this reason, when I'm walking down the street I feel the overwhelming and inexplicable urge to break into a run. It can't be ruled out that this is the very reason that María's features lost their clarity. A physicist might say: in María, the position lost its place to the moment and we know what the impetus was but we don't know what place it occupies at any given moment; or else:

María no longer obeyed the Newtonian paradigm but rather the quantum paradigm, or, better yet, that of string theory where every cybernaut is like a knot in the weft with which the social network is woven. Things that arouse a spontaneous feeling of tenderness: a puppy, scale models of cars and buildings, the pinky finger… and, in general, any manufactured miniature object. I believe men will ultimately become dispensable. This world barely tolerates those aggressive and territorial beings who prefer simple and generous sexuality in exchange for a feeling that requires the use of exhausting linguistic structures. I once overheard the following conversation between a man and a woman sitting together at a table in a cafeteria:

–You didn't want a son.
–I wanted to want one.
–That's not enough.
–Wanting one is what conceived it.
–Animals want. People love.
–I love wanting. I love the wanting of my son.
–But you don't love him.
–I want to hold him in my hands. I want to hear his crying and to see him nursing at your breast. Then I'll love him.
–I want to know what you feel.
–I don't feel anything. I feel pain when you hit me and pleasure when I enter you.
–I feel sadness. Your words make me sad.
–Words are like steel bars. They stir up feelings.
–Then I love prisons.

God kept his promise, that is, he entered the mind of Enrique, the beggar at San Andrés church, and then he told me what he saw.

For a long time Enrique had felt that something uncontrollable was churning up inside of him, giving him a dizzy feeling as if he were falling from a seven-story building, a powerful voice was calling to him, saying: Enrique, rise up and leave what little remains to you, for the richest man is he who possesses nothing. Enrique had always heard voices, voices that had accompanied him throughout his life and had helped him make the big decisions. Enrique had heard voices sitting at his desk in school, during a pleasant swim at the beach or standing in front of sale items at the supermarket. He knew that the almighty communicated with his creatures through an almost infinite chain of angels, each one whispering the divine message into the ear of the next. This extremely long chain of transmissions ultimately caused the message to reach him in the form of noise, an almost unintelligible murmur that filled him with confusion, that obliged him to use free will, something—personal liberty—to which he had never, no matter how many years passed, grown accustomed. But this time Enrique had heard the voice with perfect clarity, so he filled a suitcase with clothing and closed the door to his home, locking the keys inside.

–Does he still hear voices?
–I didn't hear anything. He spends a lot of time listening to a Walkman through giant earphones.
–Any particular program?
–Just white noise. He thinks the almighty has permanently abandoned his creation after seeing how misunderstandings of his message have ended up converting the world into a bunch of huge box stores. Something that he never foresaw. The almighty blames all this on the poor diction of his angels. He thinks the game of telephone has become a big bore.
–And the white noise?

–Enrique thinks it's the sound of the absence of God. The voice of the void. And that there's nothing better than a church for listening to that void amplified throughout the naves. San Andrés is brimming with tellurism. It's like a magnet for saintliness. San Isidro, Santa María de la Cabeza… And now, Enrique. Enrique is a kind of saint, dedicated to the void. He can spend hours glued to his Walkman, with his head raised toward the interior of the cupola, listening to the music of the void.

I like when the image of a place I once visited pops up in my memory, even if I can't quite remember where it was, something like trying to remember a dream. I fantasize about writing the story of *Lolita*, narrated by the girl herself. Time condenses in space and ends up assuming the form of a spiral: fluff, galaxies, wrinkles. 4-2-9: I know what it means. Eduardo, like almost everyone who grew up during the 1980s, went to a typing academy. In the 1980s, typing still seemed to be something of vital importance, a skill that would propel a middle-class student along a meteoric path to finding a job with a good company. Woe to whoever couldn't deftly strike the keys at more than two hundred beats per minute. Beside the keyboard of Eduardo's computer there's a typist's hand strengthener. Periodically he exercises with it to build his finger muscles in the same way as a gymnast trains daily to achieve his goals. In the fall the sky over Madrid is the same color as the slate roofs of its churches. A perfect crime is like a masterpiece. The case is archived for years until someone reopens it, someone who does not believe in giving up but rather in the incriminating fortitude of the evidence. This someone gives up again, albeit confident that another someone will come along and take up the cause after a few years or decades. Imprisoning the criminal is no longer what is most important. The statute of limitations may apply or the perpetrator may have died. What remains important is to find the clue that will provide a definitive conclusion to the enigma. Which is impossible if, indeed, it is the perfect crime. The clues don't lead to a closed solution, the pages open doors to increasingly vast spaces. We close the book and before us there remains a world inhabited by an infinite mystery. I once passed by a meeting of the Communist Party. I was on my way home after doing some shopping. A woman of about sixty years of age with the appearance of a simple housewife was speaking from a stage. She was speaking about the role of unions, of capitalism and its interest in eradicating unions through a sibylline strategy of discrediting them. I was moved. If I'd stayed for a minute longer I wouldn't have been able to hold back my tears. Within all of us there are tenants living who we know nothing about. Writing is a way of giving them a voice, of forcing them to show themselves. A city is not a physical place. A city is a collective hallucination. The beauty reflected in María's face in those photographs taken prior to her crisis of photogenicity is that of someone who is still in a prelogical condition (infantile, in an etymological sense, that is, prior to language), typical of children and certain sculptures depicting Greek divinities. A beauty that erects a transparent wall around her and protects her at the same time as it condemns her to isolation. A beauty that arouses an immediate reprographic instinct, provoking the chromosomes to flutter nervously in their cells as they fantasize a voyage beyond the body that encloses them to unite, upon aperture of the DNA zipper (performance of the familiar seduction scene), with the genes that created María's image. Eduardo can count on one hand the number of times he's felt something like passion. His minimal experience in amorous campaigns renders Eduardo clueless regarding the enamored condition. The closest he ever came to falling in love was when, while riding the train through the suburbs, he sat across from a girl. It was a yawn that caused Eduardo to notice her. Eduardo yawned.

Looking straight ahead he discovered, to his surprise, that the girl was also yawning. They yawned in unison. A coincidence by no means extraordinary. What was extraordinary was the fact that they watched each other as they yawned. Each stared into the oral cavity of the other. They exhibited, without modesty, their teeth, their glistening palates and glottises, with the spontaneous intimacy of a married couple. Thus, they mutually stripped their souls before one another through that simple yawn while, on the other side of the window there passed, at high velocity, an industrial park, an airplane descending for a landing and, in the next seat over, an old man completed his Sudoku puzzle. Eduardo could have sworn that such extraordinary emotion was not an illusion. At least, that's what he thought for a moment. He thought that such a thing would have justified, in centuries past, that a man like himself should kneel down and ask the girl for her hand in marriage. Eduardo searched the girl's eyes for encouragement. If not proof, then at least an indication, a reason for hope. The girl, however, had taken out a music player and was putting on headphones, taking extreme care of her outer ear. Eduardo saw his hopes evaporate the moment the girl began to hum and tap her foot on the rubber floor of the coach to the rhythm of the music that for him remained tragically silent. I once entered the home of my tenants in their absence. I took a shower. I turned on the coffee-maker and drank a cup of coffee seated at the table admiring their paintings and browsing some of their books. Like the magpie, I enjoy occupying other people's places, imagining myself living their lives, waking up under their sheets, wearing their clothes, strumming the strings of their guitars. The way María dries herself after peeing is by taking three sheets of toilet paper, folding them along the perforated line and folding the whole pad in half one more time. María remembers that before being fired from the modeling agency her behavior hadn't differed very much from that of an automaton's. In a swimsuit:

gather your hair back with your right hand, step forward with your right foot, raise your chin, think of yourself as a gazelle lifting its head alert to danger. In a long dress, seated on the steps of a marble staircase: *bend your elbow, draw back your shoulders, imagine you're the hood ornament on a Rolls Royce, stroke the marble as if it were an enormous, hard cock.* Fashion worked so much better the less you thought about it. Fashion was a goddess that spoke through her priests, faithful to a set of rules as rigid as the Benedictine orders (including drugs—their quantity and mode of ingestion—obeying a perfectly established ritual). Fashion was a demanding and exquisite lover that filled her with pleasure but to whom she had to subject her body, a lover who enjoyed twisting her limbs like a sadistic and jealous child with a doll. Eduardo thinks that Google Maps will be perfect when the precision of the map reaches a scale of 1:1. In that case, you could travel the world over on a life-like scale with the advantage that no one else would be around, immersed in the illusion that the world, the whole world (a sensation that Adam and Eve must have enjoyed in Paradise), is there, at your exclusive disposition. I have a special sensitivity for detecting the passage of time. Not just the months, or days, but the hours, the seconds, lapses of time that defy the faces of clocks. I feel that time passes through me. My consciousness is a kind of high speed camera capable of capturing instants of infinitesimal duration that, despite their possible beauty, make me aware of approaching death. The only means of resistance consists in trapping them, to conserve proof of their passing, like the remains of bodies strewn across a battlefield. I once knew a girl whose odor I found profoundly disagreeable. I never knew if the odor came from her body or a perfume I couldn't identify but that I associated with the odor of a decaying bouquet of flowers. It was difficult to get close to her without that odor interposing itself like an undesired and absorbent *tertius genus.* Belonging to the male sex means wanting to be the first to finish a race, wanting to reach higher to strike a ball, wanting to be published by a bigger publishing house than everybody else, wanting the most beautiful wife or girlfriend… and to reach the grave first. The spermatozoids that transport the XY chromosome are faster since they lack a part of the chromosome's burden. All in all, sex seems to be a question of speed. On certain occasions I've read a sentence I wrote but thought it was someone else's. I thought the sentence was so good that it just had to have been written by someone else. Childhood is a refuge from adulthood on a 1:3 scale in order to provide shelter to melancholy. María remembers an time when she was standing at the cash register in a clothing store. She'd bought some blue sandals just five minutes earlier. That's what she told the cashier; she said five minutes ago I bought these sandals and I want to return them. The cashier looked at her with surprise before asking her why, then, did she buy them? María became annoyed. She became very annoyed. She was on the verge of hitting the jerk with the pair of sandals. But she didn't. Instead, she thought about it, she considered things while the other customers formed a line behind her, waiting to pay for their clothes. She considered things for long enough to realize that in the end it wasn't her that had wanted to possess the sandals. A week before she'd bought a turquoise-colored scarf. It was the scarf that had wanted the sandals. María had only been a tool for one thing (the scarf) to establish a relationship with another thing (the sandals), an agent for transmitting the desires of objects for other objects. María was proud of herself for having reached this formidable conclusion all by herself, proud, moreover, of feeling herself to be in the hands of a force much greater and more powerful than herself. Possessed of this mystical sentiment, she picked up the receipt from the counter and left with the sandals in hand. Who was she, after all, to interfere with the attraction that some things may feel for other things? Beauty tends to give the impression of immutability. A beautiful woman doesn't seem to need anyone. Her chin rises, shunning any visual contact with the other beings of this world, in search of an equal that can only be found inhabiting the upper reaches, the skyscrapers, the ideal world of advertising billboards. In her presence, one feels the rejection experienced by an electron that attempts to approach an atom that will only be loyal to its atomic number. Unlike other features, beauty possesses a stable nature, like a hydrogen atom resting in a vacuum. It seems to me that women are much more degenerate than men. Far from conforming to the simple copulation of bodies, they fantasize a hypothetical fusion of souls. The Argentine accent always arouses contradictory emotions in me, a blend of pleasant purring and upsetting fervor. Whenever I hear it I sense that it's an extraterrestrial being that's speaking, an extraterrestrial who can imitate—almost—to perfection the speech of human beings. The best writers and soccer players are always Argentine. Maradona and Messi. Borges and Aira.

—I'm Argentine.

Now you know it. You think I'm joking. But god is really Argentine. A poet is someone who flees from language in order to go out and conquer another language. A poet is someone who has no mother tongue. Eduardo presses the button on his mouse. The click that comes back to him from the interface has a comforting effect on him, it fills him with calm. The flight of his cursor (ὅ: Apollo's spear, which wounds from afar) is the basic space-time unit for Eduardo, an indivisible atom, the origin of the coordinates for all his desires, an instant that is pure fire and beyond which he loses all track of consciousness. Women tend to pay attention to detail. So do I. Above all else, I pay attention to the details. When I pose in front of the camera, I never look into the lens. To look into the lens is to personalize it, to believe that there is someone watching through the diaphragm. Nothing could be more false. The diaphragm is not the pupil of any human being, especially not of whoever is holding the camera. The diaphragm is the pupil of something that goes beyond the human, an anxiety of visibility embodied by the photographic device. The camera that sets itself up and sets out walking on its tripod at the beginning of *Kino-Eye*, by Dziga Vertov. I've never understood mythomania. In real life, artists tend to be as contemptible as the average person in the street, if not more so. People should admire their works and forget about that human being who stinks, who cuts into bread lines or who does the utmost to avoid paying taxes. María remembers the parties she went to when she was still a fashion model. Exclusive parties that only allowed entry to beautiful men and women, men and women who scored higher than nine on a beauty scale ranging from one to ten, or men and women not necessarily plucked from a Hitlerian eugenic fantasy but who nonetheless made up for their low score on the beauty scale with a bulging bank account. She remembers one of those parties at which Darío, her love of the moment, offered her some MDMA. Within half an hour she could already feel the effects of the drug, that feeling of fellowship and fusion with all people and, in general, with anyone nearby. She observed her fellow partiers, liberated people thanks to their economic status. She thought about the extreme equality between them, people extracted from the catalogs of *Chicmodels* and *Fashionface*. Twins floating in the club's amniotic fluid. The MDMA provided the third leg of the revolutionary slogan: fraternity. So, María thought that the club had been transformed into the revolutionary ideal. She had to resist the urge to rip open her blouse, expose her breasts, and exhort everyone to follow her somewhere. She had to settle for secretly flashing Darío, whose smile was discombobulated by the stroboscopic lights in the ceiling. I hate when someone puts on music to "create an atmosphere." At a gathering of friends or an intimate get-together, if someone gets up to put music on, I don't know what to say, I feel awkward. On such occasions I suppose that person wants to hear something like, oh, that music is terrific, those tunes are the perfect accompaniment to our conversation. But nothing like that passes through my mind. In the fifth grade of elementary school, in honor of the principal's retirement, our grammar teacher suggested we write a poem dedicated to doña Virtudes (that was our principal's name). I had never written a poem. I've always liked challenges (during recess I liked to fight with my classmates, all of whom were bigger than me), so I wrote a poem. I remember there was a character, a kind of medieval knight who was walking toward a castle. The knight climbed over a wall and then another, and another, until he reached a courtyard that was something like the center of the castle. Then he started walking toward the heart of the courtyard and there he found a rosebush with a single flower and he stood there staring at it and the knight was satisfied and considered his quest complete, a kind of adventure whose reward was the contemplation of beauty. I remember I handed my poem in to the teacher. In fact, I was very proud of the results and I expected to be congratulated on my work. I remember standing there as the teacher read it. After she finished reading it, she put it in the pile with the rest. I returned to my seat like a seal at the aquarium who believes he's performed his best pirouette only to earn the trainer's refusal to give him a sardine. So, I thought poetry was a stupid activity. You have to write believing that the book you're writing will be the book to end all books, the book that all human generations have been patiently waiting for without knowing it, that the reader will be transformed after reading it and will go out with a flamethrower in hand prepared to incinerate everything and then proceed to reshuffle the cards of destiny. Even though we know that the world will go on as always and the only thing we'll have accomplished is to add to the already inexhaustible stock of indifference. The dots over my i's float like lofty spring clouds whereas the tails on my t's cross the post about a third of the way up. A graphologist would say that in my character there is a conflict between my adolescent dreams and a lack of willpower to make those dreams come true. I have a periodically recurring dream. In it I live in a small house, I'm aware that the house is small and I can't stop thinking that I should move to a bigger house. Until I remember that in fact there's a door that's always shut but leads to a group of rooms filled with dust that I never use. One of those rooms is a big salon that leads to a terrace. Why do I always forget that my house is big, very big? That is the question that invariably signals the end to my dream. Then I open my eyes and discover that in reality my house is quite small. Eduardo has a vague image of his body, as if it were a land with corners yet to be explored, like an Etch-A-Sketch image after you shake it up and down a couple times. Both pain and pleasure will often and unpredictably assail him, like signals sent to him from some unknown place. It wasn't until he was well into his twenties that he discovered, to his surprise, that after taking a shower a large amount of foam had accumulated beneath his scrotum. In Eduardo's life almost everything is insubstantial, banal, anodyne. Sometimes Eduardo compares himself to an aspirin. Only ten percent of every pill contains active ingredient. The rest is buffer, filler to simplify things for the stomach. No matter how much Eduardo looks to the past, no matter how many anecdotes he collects of truly transcendental experiences, that percentage still seems excessive to him for the generic medicine that constitutes his life. Perhaps the epileptic seizures, he thinks in his moments of greatest optimism, make up in some way a large part of that percentage- the remaining ninety percent- which is something that nonetheless ends up being distressing if it is examined coldly since, for all this time, he really feels absent and only someone else can account for him, just as only a neutral observer can leave for posterity the story undoubtedly filled with heroism between two adversaries who end up completely annihilated. No book is complete if it doesn't contain at least one insignificant sentence, a sentence that no reader could possibly remember because its function is the antithesis of memorable. That sentence is the ventilation shaft, the bronchus through which the world and all its inanity penetrates the text. It's the imperceptible gust of wind that causes a wave to rise up and break over the surface of the ocean and wash up on the beach. It was Darío who gave María the hamster she later named Pérez. María likes to put Pérez in her shirt pocket, to feel the hamster's soft body nestling against her breast as she walks through the house or sits at the computer. Whenever I go out and walk down the street, I check the doorway of San Andrés church where Enrique displays, on pieces of cardboard, his new compositions. Here's his latest:

> *The camel dies in the sand,*
> *The eagle on the cliff*
> *And I'd like to die, princess*
> *On your sweet lips.*

I'm mesmerized by Enrique's poems. I'd like to write poetry the way he does, without pretensions, like someone scratching his back. On the ground in front of the cardboard on which he's written his poem, there's a bowl for passersby to leave coins in appreciation of the bard's talents. Meanwhile, Enrique, a few yards away, now oblivious to his creations, shares a liter of beer with two or three brothers-in-arms. Enrique is a revelation to me as an absolutely modern artist, an artist who shows his work in an open-air museum and in return for its contemplation only asks for a symbolic contribution. The work of art as an autonomous machine whose function is to produce money. Beside Enrique, who is now joking with some young blond trans-Pyrenean tourists, I see myself as a medieval artisan who offers his craft to the public as he spins his potter's wheel. There is nothing more boring than attending a poetry reading. It's unbearable to listen to poets bleating their verses like helpless sheep. The worst thing is when they try to be modern and use some theatrical strategy to captivate their audience, which is basically made up of other poets and wannabe poets whose greatest aspiration is to earn enough in the world of poetry to be able to repeat this pathetic spectacle for the next group of aspiring poets. A vicious circle. Truly nonsense. Poetry can only be fruitful in solitude. The relationship between the poem and the reader is a relationship between you and you. To feel electricity coursing through the body all you need is a finger and an outlet. I don't understand the penchant in Spain for a poet like Ashbery. There's no young poet who not only hasn't read Ashbery but that hasn't infused his own poetry with some of the background noise and the elocutionary automatism of the New York poet. Ashbery's poetry seems to have emerged from a machine programmed by a random algorithm. You put in a coin and the machine spits out verses. I don't understand why people read Ashbery instead of buying a lawnmower. You could start the lawnmower in your living room and lie down on the couch to listen to it and tell yourself that there you have the essence of genuine poetry. Not only do objects have shadows, but concepts and ideas also have theirs. The shadow of peace, the shadow of love... I wonder what kind of shadow is cast by the idea of shadow. In the moments leading up to every epileptic seizure Eduardo's perception becomes fragmented, his vision short circuits and loses its normal continuity. The trajectory of a fly through the air becomes a discontinuous sequence like those drawings in the corners of textbooks that seem to move when you quickly flip the pages. Life splinters into still shots. Between them there are interstices in the form of flashes of light. Twelve frames per second. Ten. Five. Two. A single fixed image. A brilliance that melts the celluloid of consciousness. The pornographer I mentioned before would write in his memoirs that he finds the syncopated screams of Japanese women when they make love to be incomprehensible, as if, rather than human beings, they were dolls that emitted beeps after each thrust by the man penetrating them or as if, rather than emitting groans of pleasure, they were concentrating on making feeble, anaphrodisiac whimpers. Which is something that doesn't occur with other Asian porn actresses from China, Korea or Thailand. He can close his eyes and recognize the yowl of any actress originating from the Land of the Rising Sun. When it comes to fellatio, he deplores when a woman, with a display of prudish amateurism, draws in her lips like a toothless sexagenarian instead of proffering the more common and much more gratifying everted position like that of a fish satisfyingly caught on a hook. The pornographer likewise confesses to having passed years of his life abusing the teen section of hundreds of web pages only to have suddenly lost his sensibility and taste for those still adolescent bodies which he discovered to be completely without the least bit of spirit, engaging in sex like someone chewing gum or playing tennis, abruptly innocuous before his eyes, merely insipid semiotic material. All of a sudden allergic, having fallen from his horse on the way to Damascus... he would try to make sense of the diagnosis. The pornographer would come to realize, at some moment, that a porn actress was essentially a spiritual being, a being from another dimension, lacking flesh, pure image forged of light that appears on the screen to take possession of our bodies. Here we have the author's dedication at the beginning of *Confessions of a Pornographer*: "To Stoya and Olivia la Roche, *lenitio tumescentiae*." María uses Photoshop to open some of the photographs in which she appears. She crops them and gives the fragments the appearance of postcards. Then she attaches them to a list of thousands of people's email addresses. Each one gets a different fragment. An eye, a piece of forehead, a cheek... Eduardo, naturally, is included on this list. Eduardo saves every one of these images. Collecting them, putting them together as if they were pieces of a puzzle, Eduardo manages to form an image, albeit blurry, of María.

I ONCE SAW A LEAF FROM A TREE lying on the asphalt in a tunnel several kilometers long. Reality can't be avoided. Even if you wish it could be. Wish, oh so much. Wish, for example, that reality were not the way it is, but rather as you wish it would be. You can't deny that wishes are another kind of reality. A reality that, although it may not negate the former—the grand reality—it can be super-imposed over it, like a complement or a sticker of the sort we used to surreptitiously stick on our school desks when we were kids. The wish for something to happen creates a sphere of possibilities that expands, acquiring more and more volume until its gravitational pull ends up attracting the desired event. The sun is a cumulus of desire and each and every one of us forms part of the fantasy. No state of mind is eternal, a statement of fact that we should not for-get in those moments when we are hostage to depression. Women harbor a void within them, a void that we men are scarcely aware of and yet it profoundly attracts us. Women speculate with this void. They win or lose depending on how we view the contest. I'll never manage to solve a Rubik's cube. *The coyote*: I know what it means. Enrique becomes especially nervous in supermarkets. He goes up and down the aisles and pauses at displays where the merchandise is piled high. He's fascinated by the agglomeration of identical objects. Without being conscious of it, he's turned off by the mass production of a single product, something that has no parallel in the natural world, except in the extraordinary case of twins. The individual trees in a forest or grains of sand on a beach are insignificant because their proliferation in this case has one clear objective: the configuration of a landscape. But what Enrique sees isn't a landscape. What Enrique sees is a serial replication, the instinct to copy—gloriously satisfied—the enigma of modern art. And that's also what's responsible for his fascination and his anxiety. What Enrique doesn't know is that his internal and external agitation is not due to identity but rather difference, the infinitesimal nuance that separates one can of Coca-Cola from the next, that distinguishes one can of sardines from the one above it, a nuance that defies even the greatest expert in the game of errors. The sum of these infinitesimals, of these imperceptible perceptions, as Leibnitz theorized, ends up congregating in a single act, a single involuntary gesture, the minnow that evades the net of consciousness. Enrique, a passive agglomeration of monads, moves his lips and murmurs in front of the shelf of Asturian bean stew cans: "Like a wave, your love rolled into my life, like a wave…" Mastery is automatism. The emotion that gives rise to art derives from the recognition that deep inside this apparent automaton there is a unique human being that produces such automatism and that, at the same time, is tortured by it. Art is no longer art if it fails in both these senses. What is fascinating about a snail is not its shell, nor its soft slimy body, but rather the fact that both things coexist in a single organism. I imagine a website where people submit their secrets and, in return, for each secret submitted, the screen displays a secret provided by some unknown person. It's astounding to see how many beautiful women wander through the galleries at art fairs. None of them are artists. The artists, with the exception of certain pop stars, are generally men and women who are quite ugly and insignificant relative to their art. I've reached the conclusion that physical beauty and glamour circulate around art, an orbit dictated by the force of the paintings, the sculptures and the video installations. The spectators' beautiful bodies are a denial and a challenge to Art. They pause in front of a sculpture and they think that they are the ones who should be on display, that they incarnate the fantasy that motivates the manufacture of all these monstrosities.

> *I'm the one who causes disorder*
> *the one in the supermarket who changes the placement*
> > *of cans*
>
> *the one who undermines surveys*
> *the one who sometimes behaves erratically to*
> *better be confused with nature*
> *the one who in the equation of words*
> > *and things*
> *always adds an unknown.*

I always wanted to end a book with a poem. Although at times you should know when to act against your desires. When people gather in front of the counter at the departure gate, when a crowd gets excited because their team won or because they feel threatened, I am unmoved by the stimulus, I become an observer of the masses. This ability to remain apart, together with my gifts for observation, would have made me a spectacular sociologist, if I'd had the slightest interest in sociology. There are people who air their ideas exactly as if they were taking their dog out for a walk, firmly secured on a leash. They show them off, they let them play with other ideas. They sniff each other. They bark. They bark a lot. Some will bite if you let them off their leash. In public restrooms, the urinals in the center are almost always free. Jim Morrison's superciliary arches. I'm less concerned with society than with order, less concerned with correctness than with syntax. There's no reason why darkness has to be associated with the night. A flock of birds sitting on a wire could represent darkness just as much as, or more than, a room with the lights turned off during the night. Feelings are not always manifest in a continuous way. Sometimes it's a discreet sum of stimuli that leads to our happiness or discomfort- Eduardo, for example, in María's wig boutique. His interaction with any one of those wigs, exhibited on its impersonal bust, left Eduardo feeling something between fascination and indifference. Nonetheless, the sheer number of wigs, the almost infinite variety of colors and textures, overwhelmed him with an anxiety that was difficult to deal with. Eduardo tried to concentrate his attention on a blond wig that was modeled on Kim Novak's hairstyle in *Vertigo*. He noticed it the first time he passed by the shop's display window. He always thought that kind of hairdo, in the form of a spiral, was like a wormhole that made it possible to travel through time, the way Madeleine, the female protagonist of *Vertigo*, would metamorphose into Carlotta Valdés just by putting a bow on top. And now, there was Kim Novak in front of him, returned from the dead. That day María had her hair put up and although it wasn't in the same spiral form that had immortalized Kim Novak, the likeness of the two was quite disconcerting. María didn't know that the man who was offering her a hairpiece of inferior quality in exchange for the *Vertigo* wig was Eduardo. Eduardo didn't know that the salesgirl in that boutique, who could pass for a revived Madeleine, was really María. Eduardo took Santiago Carrillo's hairpiece out of a supermarket shopping bag. It's really Carrillo's hairpiece, I inherited it from my father. María realized at first glance that this man was impaired. Just like herself—so she imagined—a human being with extensive experience in the field of adversity, a catalyzer for compassion. The hairpiece was disgusting. Nonetheless, his curls, Eduardo's curls, appealed to María. Perhaps the hairpiece was genuine. She smiled at him. "I propose a trade. I'll give you this museum piece and in exchange you give me that wig (with his free hand Eduardo pointed at Madeleine's wig). I'm offering you a piece of our country's history. Something extremely valuable." Eduardo held up the hairpiece as if it was the Golden Fleece itself. María didn't know what to say. Eduardo had nothing else to offer. He went to the bust and picked up the wig. In turn, he covered the bust's bald head with Carrillo's rag. He weighed the blond hair in his hands. The bundle in the form of a spiral was perfect. With the skill of experience, he put the wig on. He heard the salesgirl's laughter behind him. It must have meant that she'd accepted his offer. Eduardo wasn't mistaken. If Eduardo had only been a little more gifted in the affairs of the heart he would have realized that they were now positioned to enter into flirtatious conversation and that, therefore, not to do so could only be understood as an act of rejection or, even worse, of cowardice. When I was a kid I was obsessed with flying saucers. When I was fifteen years old I drew on the last page of my physics and chemistry notebook a blueprint for making one. Later I discovered that outer space is everywhere and that words describe it better than any complex blueprints. I've seen the films of Haneke. I've seen the films of Pasolini. I've read de Sade and Bernhard. In this life I can no longer suffer very much. At night, the same day that Eduardo had gone to her boutique, María scanned the hairpiece worn by Santiago Carrillo and saved it to the folder called, *Scanned things that look like a dandelion seed after being caught between two fingers.*

Your Words Matter

Your Words Matter

Your Words Matter